MASTER CROOK'S CRIME ACADEMY

ROBBERY FOR RASCALS

Look out for more escapades

MASTER CROOK'S CRIME ACADEMY
BURGLARY FOR BEGINNERS
CLASSES IN KIDNAPPING

MASTER CROOK'S CRIME ACADEMY

ROBBERY FOR RASCALS

A BOOK THIS FUNNY
SHOULD BE
AGAINST THE LAW!

FROM THE
BEST-SELLING
AUTHOR OF
HORRIBLE HISTORIES™

TERRY DEARY

Illustrated by John Kelly

■SCHOLASTIC

For Ken Dargue and Michael Piggins,
who taught me all I know about driving a
steam locomotive.

First published in the UK in 2009 by Scholastic Children's Books
An imprint of Scholastic Ltd
Euston House, 24 Eversholt Street
London, NW1 1DB, UK
Registered office: Westfield Road, Southam, Warwickshire, CV47 0RA
SCHOLASTIC and associated logos are trademarks and or registered trademarks
of Scholastic Inc.

ISBN 978 1 407 11016 5

Printed and bound in the UK by CPI Mackays, Chatham, ME5 8TD
Papers used by Scholastic Children's Books are made
from wood grown in sustainable forests.

1 3 5 7 9 10 8 6 4 2

This is a work of fiction. Names, characters, places, incidents and dialogues are
products of the author's imagination or are used fictitiously. Any resemblance to
actual people, living or dead, events or locales is entirely coincidental.

www.scholastic.co.uk/zone

CONTENTS

Before word

Yes, I remember 1837 as clearly as if it were yesterday. I know! I know, it was sixty-four years ago now. But I kept a diary at the time. I always knew that I would have to tell the story one day.

Now the old queen is dead. Not before time, some might say. She came to the throne in 1837 and soon afterwards they named the rest of the century after her. The Victorian Age, they called it.

Now she's dead and her son, fat Prince Edward has become King Edward the seventh. I suppose they will call this the Edwardian Age!

Everyone said they were sorry to lose old Queen Victoria. But they have a funny way of showing it!. We've had parties in the street, bonfires with roasting potatoes, fireworks and sweets for the children. I have to say, there has also been a lot of beer for the grown-ups.

But why am I talking about the dead queen and the new king? What I was trying to say is that I am turning the strange story of 1837 into a book. I can tell the tale now that we are in a new age and no one can be hurt by it.

Do not ask who I am. I won't tell you. But believe me, I was there. I know.

It all happened up in the busy, bleak, blustery and barbarous town of Wildpool, up on the north-eastern coast of England. I lived through it so I know these things are true. Amazing . . . unbelievable, even . . . but as true as I am sitting here scratching away with my favourite pencil.

You won't have heard this story because it took place in a poor and forgotten town. I always call Wildpool "a midden that's hidden".

I started my story in January of that fateful year.

That has already been published in the first book, Burglary for Beginners. You may have read it? But no matter. This story is just as sensational, and you may meet several of the characters who appeared in Burglary for Beginners, so if you haven't read the first book don't worry. I won't worry! Because I know you WILL read it when you have read this terrifically true tale.

But February had its own mysterious tale to tell. A tale of steaming, screaming trains and tracks and a vile villain that robbed the poor to make himself rich.

At the dark heart of the story is Master Crook's

Crime Academy. A school that teaches the tricks of the criminal trade to the young.

"Shocking!" you cry. "What a scandal! A school that teaches children to cheat, boys to burgle and girls to gurgle!"

I don't know why I said that. Does that ever happen to you? You are writing something sensible then your pencil runs off and writes something of its own? The girls in this story don't "gurgle". They do many curious things but gurgling isn't one of them. Can you forget I said that? Thank you.

"Aha!" I cry. "All is not what it seems at Master Crook's Academy. Wait and see. Or, as the ship's captain said when he threw the anchor overboard . . . 'weight and sea'."

I will keep you waiting no longer. I told you this story is set in 1837. I misled you. (Never trust a writer.) It really began forty years before that fateful date. Years before the old queen was even born. Years before I was born. The years when our humble country was at war with France and mighty warships were built on the river at Wildpool.

So, I wasn't there myself, but I have spoken to a man who WAS there. Who was a young man in the year of 1797 at the start of our tale. . .

A tale of fear, of fortune and of Fumble.

Mr X

28 February 1901

Writers who hide their name say they are writing under a "nom de plume". That's French – and it is all right to use French since we beat them in that war. Anyway, "nom de plume" means "name of pen" . . . a name they only use when they are holding the writing tool. Since I don't use a pen I do not have a "nom de plume". I have a "nom de pencil".

Chapter 1

CARRIAGE AND COURT

Wildpool Moor – 16th February 1797

The wind blew wildly across the moor and a young man shivered as he huddled in the bare bushes. His coat was thin and his boots more holey than a priest.

He wore a cloak and thought it made him look like the famous Dick Turpin. In fact the cloak was a grey blanket that he'd tied with a ribbon – it made him look like a scarecrow.

Cold mud seeped through the sole of his right boot. "I'm going to buy some new boots when I've done this robbery," he promised himself. It cheered him up. His pinched face suddenly glowed with joy. "And *socks*!" he moaned. "I've *always* wanted a pair

of socks. Ooooooh! And stockings for my mum too.
And a wig. . .

A wig for him, not his mum, he should have
said. His mother had enough hair. It flowed all
the way down her back. None on her head, but
plenty on her back.

. . . all the best highwaymen have a wig with a black
hat with three corners. My name will bring terror to
the roads round Wildpool, just as Dick Turpin's did in
the south."

But his name would bring only laughter to the
people of Wildpool. For his name wasn't Dick Turpin.
It was Rick Turnip. He was almost the last of a long line
of Turnips. Their roots went back into the mists of time.

That's a joke by the way . . . roots . . .
turnip . . . see? I didn't say it was a good
joke so don't groan like that.

Fifty years before, Tom Turnip had been a
terror. The Turnip families still had his picture on the
walls of their cottages. They were proud of him.

WANTED

DEAD OR ALIVE
(OR SOMETHING IN BETWEEN)

TOM TURNIP – THE ONE ARMED BANDIT
WANTED FOR
RUNNING UP BEHIND LADIES IN THE STREET
PINCHING THEIR PURSES (OR PINCHING THEIR
BOTTOMS IF THEY DON'T HAND OVER THEIR PURSE)
THIS MAN IS ARMED. IN FACT HE HAS ONE ARM.
THE OTHER ARM IS A WOODEN ONE.
(HE STOLE IT FROM A SECOND-HAND SHOP.)

REWARD OF HALF A CROWN
FOR HIS CAPTURE

He was a legend in the Turnip family. "Tom Turnip. The man they couldn't capture!"

That wasn't *quite* true. He *was* captured when he tried to escape from a tavern with a cheese sandwich. A cheese sandwich that he hadn't paid for.

The law officer found our sandwich-stealing Tom hiding in a ditch; he put irons around his wrist and chained him to the village pump while he went to fetch the magistrate.

When the officer returned Tom Turnip's arm was still fastened to the pump . . . but Tom wasn't fastened to the arm. It was his *false* arm and he simply unfastened it and ran off.

Tom met his doom when he tried to cross the river on some slippery stepping stones and fell in. It's hard to swim with just one arm. . .

Well, to be honest Tom had never learned to swim when he had two arms so he hand NO chance.

. . .his body was washed out to sea and never seen again.

The Turnip family believed their Tom had escaped to America where he made a living robbing

stagecoaches. That thought made them very happy.

The law officer handed the wooden arm back to the owner of the second-hand shop, so the shop-owner was happy too.

The Turnips said, "Tom was a dangerous outlaw."

The law officer said, "No, he was 'armless."

THIS was the man that Rick Turnip has grown up hearing stories about. And stories are dangerous things. Rick wanted to BE Tom Turnip – highwayman.

You will be delighted to hear he had no plans to copy Tom's bad habit of pinching ladies' bottoms. Just as well. He wasn't nippy enough! Hah! Pinch . . . nip . . . nippy? Geddit? Oh, never mind.

One night, in the Black Sheep Inn, he overheard the Twitch Family gang plotting an evil plot. "Tomorrow," they plotted, "Lord Fumble leaves Fumble Hall for his country house . . . Wishington Country Manor."

"So?"

"So whenever he goes from house to house he takes the Fumble Family Fortune with him on his coach."

"So?"

9

"So, we stop the coach, make him hand over the gold and make ourselves very rich!"

"How rich?"

"I just told you . . . *very*!"

Rick Turnip smiled a secret smile. He decided he would beat the Twitch Family at their own game and rob the coach *before* they had the chance. He knew the rutted road Lord Fumble would take so all he had to do was hide in the bushes . . .

Which is where we had left him before you got me talking about old Tom Turnip!

Rick had no idea what time the coach would arrive. He was up at dawn and had waited all day without even a cheese sandwich to eat. He made his mouth go very watery, just thinking, "I wonder what happened to Tom Turnip's cheese sandwich that he nicked? I bet the law officer ate it!"

But as morning turned to afternoon he heard the clip-clop, clip-clop, clop-clop, flip-flop, clop-clip, flip-clip, flop-clop of carriage horses. (It was a very rutted road and that made it hard for the horses to clip and clop correctly.)

The carriage was the very latest 1798 model . . .
even though the year was 1797, the carriage makers
liked to boast it was *next* year's "model". That's how
they sold it to their rich customers . . .

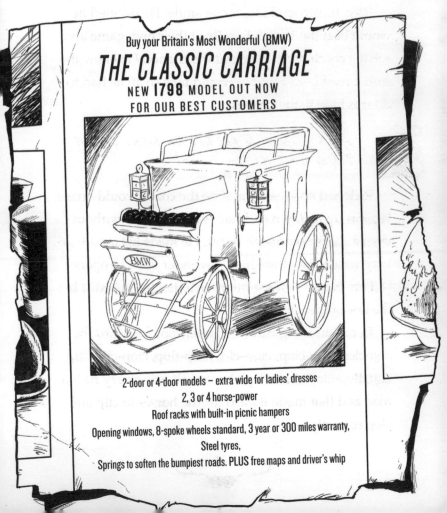

Buy your Britain's Most Wonderful (BMW)

THE CLASSIC CARRIAGE
NEW 1798 MODEL OUT NOW
FOR OUR BEST CUSTOMERS

2-door or 4-door models – extra wide for ladies' dresses
2, 3 or 4 horse-power
Roof racks with built-in picnic hampers
Opening windows, 8-spoke wheels standard, 3 year or 300 miles warranty,
Steel tyres,
Springs to soften the bumpiest roads. PLUS free maps and driver's whip

The young man blew his nose on his handkerchief then fastened it round the lower half of his face.

He stepped out into the road and placed his finger under his grey cloak to make it look as if he had a gun.

Most highwaymen carried a pistol. Dick Turpin did. Rick Turnip didn't. Guns cost money. Once he'd robbed Lord Fumble he thought he'd go out and buy a pistol . . . after he'd bought socks, of course.

He raised his finger under the cloak. "Stand and deliver! Your money or your life!"

A shiver ran up through Rick Turnip's spine then back down again to where it started. "Ooooh!" he breathed. "I've always wanted to say that."

The coach stopped. The window slid down and the handsome young Lord Fumble stuck his handsome head out that was topped with a handsome hat. "What have we stopped for *now*, James?"

"Another highwayman, your grace," the driver said.

"Highwayman? Highwayman? Where's his horse?" the lord roared.

The driver turned to Rick. "His lordship wants to know where your horse is."

"I haven't got a horse!" Rick laughed in scorn. "I'm not made of money."

"He says he's not made of money . . ." the driver began to say.

"I heard! I heard, you ninny." The lord opened the door and stood on the step of the carriage. His suit was of finest blue satin with silver stitching and his socks were as white as snowdrops. "You can't be a highwayman without a horse, you rascal. You're a footpad. Nothing but a common *footpad*. What are you? Well? What are you?"

"Erm . . . a footpad, my lord," Rick muttered miserably.

"Who do you think you are, calling yourself a highwayman? Who do you *think* you are? Eh? Dick Turpin?"

"No. Rick Turnip."

"Ah! Make a note of his name, driver. Rick Turnip, he says. We know your name. You may as well tell us where you live."

"I'm not telling you that! Do I *look* stupid?" Rick cried.

"How do I know if you look stupid if I can't see your face. You may have the most stupid face in the north for all I know."

"Well I haven't!" Rick cried and tore off the handkerchief.

"Jolly good, now we know what you look like. You'll be arrested. And I don't like footpads on my estate. I have them arrested and hanged, do you hear? Hanged! Drive on, driver!"

"Stop, put up your hands or I'll shoot!" Rick called.

The driver dropped the reins and raised his hands.

The young and handsome lord pulled a blunderbuss from the coach. "That's what that bunch of ruffians down the road said," he explained. "But I shot first. And my gun was packed with all sorts of scrap metal. You should have seen them run, pulling bits of old candlesticks out of their backsides! Hah!"

Rick smiled slowly. "Ah! So it's not loaded *now* then, *is* it?"

Young Lord Fumble's handsome young face turned pale. "Ah . . . no . . . well. . ."

"So hand over the gold, please, or I shoot!" the footpad said politely.

To be honest it's easy to be polite when you are pointing a gun at somebody. It is harder to be polite when (say) a stranger's dog bites your leg in the street. I mean, it is hard to say, "Excuse me, sir, but could I trouble you to remove your little pet's teeth from my leg? It is rather uncomfortable." It is much easier to say something impolite like "* !***%.!*%.!%.!*"

Lord Fumble threw the gun into the ditch and sighed. "Get the gold off the roof, driver, and hand it over. A bullet could do a lot of damage to my handsome face, you know."

Rick Turnip's heart was fluttering like a wasp's wing. He was so near to being a hero like the family's famous Tom. So close to owning his first pair of socks. So close . . . and yet so far.

The Turnips have never been very lucky. So, at that moment, a gust of wind whipped at Rick's blanket-cloak and whisked it away from his pointing finger.

"Aha!" Lord Fumble said with a laugh like a donkey. "You haven't got a gun at all. You just have a finger. Driver . . . don't give this foul footpad a penny."

"But he'll shoot me!" the coach driver whined.

"With his finger?"

"You never know, my lord, the finger might be loaded," the man objected. "It's me that gets it if he's foot-padding around with a loaded finger!"

Lord Fumble frowned at Rick Turnip. "Is that a loaded finger you are pointing at my driver?"

"Well, to be honest, my lord, I couldn't afford a gun OR the powder or the bullets."

"See, driver?" Fumble sneered. "You've been frightened by a finger. Now, arrest that man and we'll take him to Wildpool court, give him a fair trial, find him guilty and hang him."

Rick Turnip saw his plot going horribly wrong and decided it would be a good time to leave. He turned and began to creep towards the bushes. "Stop that man!" Lord Fumble cried.

A moment later the coach driver's whip flicked out and the thin leather wrapped itself around Rick's skinny neck. The driver hauled him back towards the coach, used some of the baggage rope to tie his hands then fastened it to the back of the coach.

Rick was forced to walk behind the coach to Wildpool and his fate. He stumbled over the February mud till at last they reached the courthouse. He was

17

led to a cell and given some hot soup and fresh bread. It was the best meal he'd eaten. Ever.

After an hour Rick was led up to the court and chained to a screen that ran around a platform. This was called the "dock".

The clerk of the court was a fussy little man with spectacles and a bald head. "Court will rise for the judge!"

The few people who were in court stood up and a door behind the judge's bench opened. In walked the judge.

"Here!" Rick cried. "I've seen you before!"

"Silence in court," Judge Fumble growled. "What are the charges?"

"Armed highway robbery, your honour," the clerk said.

"Do you plead guilty?" Lord Fumble asked as he pushed the long horse-hair wig in place.

"Not really. I mean, I wasn't *armed* and I didn't rob nothing, did I?" the accused man shrugged.

"You tried to get money through menaces. That's a crime. You admitted it so you are guilty," Lord Fumble said.

Oh, that sounds too, too harsh, doesn't it? But I have to tell you it is close to the truth. In 1833 a court report showed that most trials lasted just seven or eight minutes. The guilty were hanged within a couple of days. Some people now, in 1901, still call the 1830s "the good old days". Good for rope-makers maybe.

He reached under his desk and pulled out a black square of cloth. He placed it on his head and read from a card with a black edge. "The court orders you to be taken from here to the place from where you came, and then to the place of execution, and that you be hanged by the neck until you are dead, and that your body be afterward be buried within the grounds of the prison in which you shall be held. And may the Lord have mercy on your soul."

Lord Fumble read it in a bored voice and stood up.

"Sorry, my lord," the clerk said quickly, "but you cannot hang a man for trying to get money with menaces."

"I can when it's me he was menacing," the judge said, in a menacing voice.

"The law won't allow it!"

Fumble sat down heavily. "What CAN I do to him then?"

"Forty days in prison, my lord."

He passed a sheet of paper to the judge who pulled a quill pen from an ink pot and scratched on the paper.

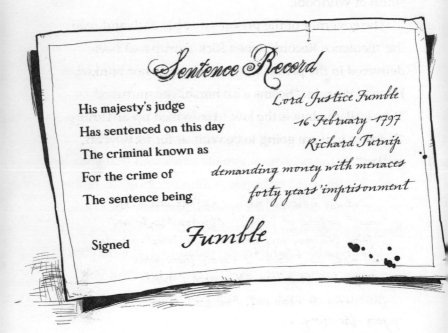

Sentence Record

His majesty's judge	*Lord Justice Fumble*
Has sentenced on this day	*16 February 1797*
The criminal known as	*Richard Turnip*
For the crime of	*demanding money with menaces*
The sentence being	*forty years' imprisonment*
Signed	*Fumble*

"Take him down," the judge ordered and passed the record card to the law officer who stood by the door.

"The court will rise!" the bald clerk cried quickly but Lord Fumble was out of the door before anyone could move.

And that is how Rick Turnip ended up in the great grey fortress that was Darlham Gaol, twenty miles south of Wildpool.

The governor of the prison sat at his desk and read the "Sentence Record" when Rick Turnip had been delivered in the prison wagon. The governor blinked. He read it again. "Seems a bit harsh," he muttered. "Oh, well, the law is the law." He looked up at Turnip. "It seems you are going to be with us for forty years, my lad!"

Did Lord Fumble make a mistake and write "years" instead of "days"? Maybe. Maybe not. I think this may just have been his cruel revenge. But what do I know? I wasn't there when Turnip went to prison. Of course I WAS there when he came out. And that's where he joins the story. . .

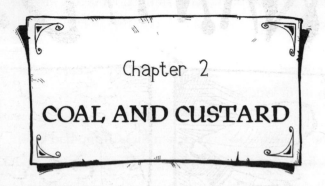

Chapter 2

COAL AND CUSTARD

Wildpool Town – Tuesday 14th February 1837

Master Crook's Crime Academy was a large house, on Wildpool High Street. A warm coal fire crackled in the grate. Two of its three pupils sat at their tables waiting for lessons to begin.

Smiff Smith was a rough-haired, thin-faced boy with eyes as sly as a dog-snatcher in a poodle parlour full of puppies. He was drawing a poster. . .

WANT!D!

SMIFF SMITH
For being the most
famous highway robber
that ever lived
Handsome and brave
A gentleman of the road
Public enemy number 2
Reward for his capture
DEAD OR ALIVE
1 penny

ALICE WHITE
For being the
scariest girl ever to
have lived
Ugly and smelly
A lady of your nightmares
Public enemy number 1
Reward for her capture
DEAD OR DEAD
1000 guineas

The girl at the other table was Alice White, a pinch-faced girl with curling fair hair and wild eyes.

But she was not at all as twist-faced and cross-eyed as Smiff Smith's pictures showed. My Uncle Joseph's in-growing toenail wasn't as ugly as that. If Alice had seen the sketch Smiff would have had an in-growing nose. Know what I mean?

"What you doing, Smiff?" she asked.

He shrugged and hid the picture. "Just drawing a wanted poster for myself."

"What are you wanted for?" Alice asked.

"For being the most famous highway robber ever!" he said.

She scowled at him. "Have you ever tried highway robbery?" she asked.

"No . . . but that's what we're here for . . . to learn!" he said.

A tall man with gooseberry-green eyes that bulged a little entered the room. His thin moustache was stiff with wax but his fingers flowed like water in a fountain. "Good morning, class," he said.

"Good morning, Mr Dreep. Are you going to teach us how to be highway robbers?" Smiff asked. "Robbing stagecoaches? They're the crooks that get their names in the newspapers! And I want to be famous."

The teacher shook his head slowly. "They usually get in the newspapers because they are being executed. They've been caught."

"I wouldn't get caught!" Smiff argued.

"Who says, you says?" Alice jeered.

"Not if we learn from a real highwayman," Smiff answered. "What about it, Mr Dreep?"

"Hmm!" the teacher said and spread his rippling fingers. "Maybe Master Crook knows someone who will make a good teacher. I'll ask him. Meanwhile we'll get on with today's lesson   stealing sausages to feed the old and helpless."

Smiff sighed. "I'll never get famous as a sausage stealer."

"And you may not end up on the gallows," Samuel Dreep told him. "Now . . . step one . . . first: Spot Your Sausage. . ."

*

The February wind whistled wickedly through the town, just as it had forty years before when Rick Turnip had been arrested.

It was even colder in the home of Maximus Mixly. The tiny Mixly twins stood in front of the fire and gazed in wonder at a wooden frame on the mantelpiece.

You are probably thinking this was a very dangerous thing to do. Children should not stand in front of a fire unless there is a fireguard in place. And you would be right . . . usually. But this fire was made up of coal dust and glowed no warmer than a candle. They were safe, trust me.

Millie and Martin stared at the printed paper in the wooden frame as if it were a plate of hot apple pudding covered in custard.

This may seem odd to you when you see the paper. . .

This is to certify that *Maximus Mixly*
Is the owner of *ONE* share in
The Wildpool and Helton Railway
to the value of
One Thousand Pounds

"Yes, my children," Mrs Mixly said. "That is all our fortune. Your father paid everything we own and borrowed more from the bank to buy that!"

Millie looked at Martin and then at her mother. "Can we eat it?"

"No, my darling, it is far too precious to eat!"

"So when WILL we get something to eat, Mama?" Martin asked. He was a short, thin child with a face like a mouse.

You know I mean it was a thin and pointed face with little bright eyes, like a mouse. I don't mean it was covered in grey fur and had long whiskers sticking out of the side of the nose. That would be plain ridiculous.

"It is dinner time at the Johnson house next door. Soon they will be finished. The cook will scrape the leftovers into the bin . . . and you, my darlings, can help yourselves."

"Thank you, Mama," Millie said with a sigh. She also had the face of a mouse. A very hungry mouse. In fact if these children HAD been mice they would have not been afraid of cats. They were so hungry they would have eaten any cat that came near . . . whiskers and all.

"Mama," Martin said. "Could we not *sell* the paper in the frame for a thousand pounds. Then we could buy our own food and not have to eat it cold from the Johnsons' bin?"

Mrs Mixly shook her head sadly and stirred the coal dust till it smoked a little. "Lord Fumble has built the Wildpool and Helton Railway."

She pointed to a small map that lay on the table.

28

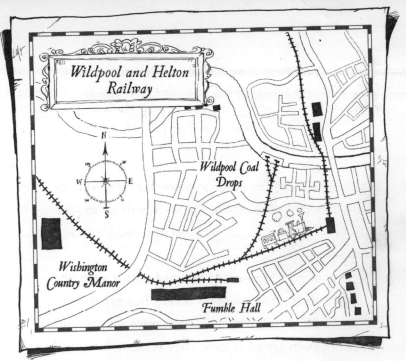

Mrs Mixly explained. "His lordship built it by selling a thousand shares at a thousand pounds a time . . . that is a million pounds. Think of that."

"Yes, but all we have is a piece of paper. Paper we can't even eat!" Millie moaned.

Mrs Mixly nodded. "The railway line runs from the coal mine at Helton to the coal ships on the river Wildpool," she explained. "It also has a branch line that joins Fumble Hall to Wishington Country Manor."

"I've seen the trains," Martin cried. "They are

beautiful. One day, when we are rich, I am going to buy a book and collect the numbers of the trains. I will be a trains-potter!"

Millie looked at him sourly. "Martin. There are only two trains on the line. Number 2 and Number 3.

In case you are wondering what happened to Number 1 I have to tell you that, sadly, its boiler burst and it exploded. Engines did that a lot back in 1837. The explosion was a terrible loss to the trains-potters of Wildpool. It was an even greater loss to the engine driver's wife as her husband was blown into little pieces.

They won't take a lot of potting." She looked at her mama. "So we own a little bit of Wildpool and Helton Railway?"

"Yes, my dear."

"Which bit?"

"I . . . I don't know."

"Can't we SELL it and eat?"

"No one wants it. The railway is only used to carry coal. It only makes money for Lord Fumble," Mrs Mixly said. Millie opened her mouth to ask a question but her mama got in first. "But ONE day the line will join with the Great Northern Line . . . a railway line that will carry people from England to Scotland in a day. When Wildpool and Helton Railway joins it then everyone will want to ride on the railway. Our one share will be worth TEN thousand pounds! We'll be rich! Rich! Rich, and all because of our precious share," she said dusting the wooden frame carefully with her handkerchief.

"I'd rather have an apple pudding," Martin muttered.

"With steaming custard," his sister added. "Come on, Martin, let's see what's in the bin next door."

Darlham Gaol – Wednesday 15th February 1837

The governor of Darlham Prison sat behind his desk. Old Rick Turnip stood in front of it. "Good morning, Rick, how are you?"

"Very well, Charlie. There are some new books coming in the library today – a new one by that Walter Scott. I love his books. Lots of criminals like that Rob Roy and the Pirate. I read them all before I let the prisoners borrow them!" Rick chuckled.

Rick Turnip was forty years older than when we left him in the courtroom, he was better fed and wore a neat uniform and strong boots. He even had socks – THREE pairs. It was a good life.

"We have had a visit from the famous Elizabeth Fry," the governor said. "You have heard of her?"

"Heard of her? Why, I've read her book *Prisons in Scotland and the North of England* many times. A great lady!"

You can still buy this book today. But it is not so exciting as a Master Crook's Crime Academy

book. I am a very modest person. Really. But Elizabeth Fry was great at changing the cruel world of the old prisons. But she was not a great writer. I am.

"Yes, well she has looked into some of the cases and showed a special interest in yours. It seems she was very angry that you've been locked away for forty years for a crime that was only worth forty days."

Turnip shrugged. "Not exactly *locked away*, Charlie. I mean, I learned to read, you gave me a wonderful job looking after the library, you send me out most days to buy your tobacco and newspaper. It's been a good life. I'm not complaining."

The governor was a flabby man in a slightly scruffy grey suit and dirty fingernails. He waved a grubby hand at Turnip now. "And we have loved having you. But your sentence ends tomorrow. Mrs Fry has arranged for you to be released. You are free to go, Rick. A whole day early too! Isn't that good news?"

He passed a piece of paper across the table. Turnip read it. . .

Discharge Papers

This to certify the convict *Rick Turnip* has served his sentence at Darlham Gaol. He is hereby released into the world. Governor Charles Hope has graded this prisoner as *Class 1*

Comment: *Rick Turnip is the most honest convict I have ever met and a lovely bloke. I would trust him with my life. I hope someone will trust him with a job. He is a credit to Darlham Gaol*

Charles Hope. 15 February 1837

The footpad frowned. His lips wobbled but it took a while for the words to come. "Go, Charlie? Go where?"

"Anywhere you want. Home!"

"But this is my home," the old convict said. "Mother died twenty years ago . . . you let me go to her funeral. But her house was just rented. I mean . . . I've nowhere else to go."

"Have you no family?" the governor asked.

"Mum had a brother that lived near to us in Wildpool. He's dead but he had children and

grandchildren, I think. But I've never met them."

The governor reached into his pocket and pulled out some money. "In a way, Rick, you have been like a servant to me since I got here thirty years ago. I never paid you. . ."

"I never expected payment, Charlie. I was happy."

"No, but I feel it's my duty to lend you some money to set you on your way," the governor said. "Here are a couple of guineas. When you get yourself a job then you can pay me back."

Turnip picked up the money slowly. "Thanks, Charlie. You are all heart. All heart."

"Clear out your cell, we have a couple of sheep rustlers coming in this morning." The man stretched out a grubby and flabby hand. "Good luck, Rick. We'll all miss you. The way you looked after new criminals was marvellous. Helped them settle in, made them feel a bit less frightened. Yes. We'll miss you. Goodbye."

Turnip shook the governor's hand firmly. He sniffed away a tear and nodded goodbye.

An hour later the old highwayman was standing on the cobbles outside the prison gates and wondering which way to turn. He carried a small bundle with

a blanket, a little food and his spare socks, his two
guineas and a favourite book.

There was a small market in the town square that
was a wriggling riot of noisy animals being bought
and sold.

*The animals were not just noisy. They were
also very smelly. Where there are animals there
are animal droppings. If you ever go to a farm
market be very careful where you put your
feet.*

A farm worker was struggling to load a pig on to
his cart. Turnip hurried across to him, grabbed the
back legs of the pig and hoisted it, squealing and
kicking, into the old wooden cart.

The sweating farm worker had more mud and
sweat on his face than the pig had on her whole body.
He grinned and showed gaps where other pigs had
kicked out his teeth. "Thank you, mate. You're a brick.
Anything I can do for you?"

"You could give me a ride," Turnip said.

"You don't know where I'm going."

"Neither do I," Turnip said with a shrug.

"I'm off to the piggery at Helton . . . five miles south of Wildpool. Do you know it?" the farm hand asked as he prodded the pony into life and creaked and clattered out of the market square.

"I haven't been to Wildpool for forty years. I think I may have family there," the ex-convict said. "It's as good a place to start a new life as anywhere," he said.

"A lot will have changed in forty years!" the driver chuckled. "You won't know the place."

For Rick Turnip, more had changed than he had imagined. He had *heard* about the railways in the newspapers and seen drawings of them. But when they neared Helton coal pits he saw one for the first time.

The cart stopped at a crossing and let a coal train roar through.

It was a fire-breathing monster, like a mechanical dragon. The noise shook Turnip and drowned even the squeals of the frightened pig. He gasped as clouds of choking smoke swallowed the cart. "It's on fire! Quick! Put it out!"

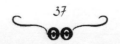

"Nah! The fire heats the water and makes the steam. The steam drives the piston and the engine pulls the coal wagons."

"You seem to know a lot about these trains, my friend," Turnip said as he wiped the sooty smoke off his face.

"I do! I am a trains-potter. I pots the train numbers in my book."

"How many have you got?"

"BOTH of them!" the farmhand said proudly.

"There are only two?"

"Well, there were three till No. 1 blew up. But one day soon this line will join with the Great Northern Line and we'll see dozens. I'll be ready with me notebook when they come."

The pony pulled the cart over the track and the petrified pig stopped shaking.

Of course, if the pig knew what was going to happen to her when she reached the butcher shop she would have been even more worried. But she had never heard of the dreadful word "bacon". And, if you ever meet a pig, it would be kinder not to tell them about butcher shops, ham

sandwiches, chops and pork pies. If the pig
asks you then it's kinder to lie. Tell it porkies.

"Here we are!" the farmhand cried. "Helton
Colliery."

Rick Turnip looked around and shivered. But it
wasn't the February wind that chilled his bones.

Chapter 3

PUDDING AND POLICEMEN

Wildpool Town – Wednesday 15th February 1837

Mrs Mixly looked at a sign hanging on a green gate.

MASTER CROOK'S CRIME ACADEMY

Tuition for the children of the poor to help them stay out of prison.

She was pale as a February frost and looked as worried as a cat in a dogs' home. She rapped at the

door. After a minute the door was opened by a boy with a shining face and spiked dark hair. "Hello, madam. Master Crook's Crime Academy at your service."

The woman threw a worried glance over her shoulder, cleared her throat and spoke quickly.

You should be very careful to look before you throw anything over your shoulder. Someone may be standing behind you and they could be seriously hurt. Especially if it's a horseshoe. Throwing a horseshoe over your left shoulder is lucky. But unlucky for someone walking behind. Being hit by a worried look is not so painful.

"I wonder if I could see Master Crook . . . or do I need an appointment?"

The boy pulled a face. "I can *ask* . . . but you can't see him. Nobody *sees* him. I've been here a month and I haven't seen him yet. I've spoken to him a few times though."

"How do you do that if you can't see him?"

"I either talk down the speaking tube. Or if he has a

tricky job for me he sometimes tells me about it down in the cellar – it's dark and he's behind a curtain."

"How strange!"

"He's a strange man . . . but brilliant! Come this way," the boy said and led the way into the house. "My name's Smiff, by the way. Who shall I say is calling?"

"Mrs Mixly," the woman said.

Smiff led the way into a pleasant living room with comfortable chairs. A girl was dusting ornaments. She was a moon-faced, pleasant girl.

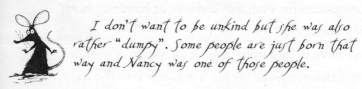

I don't want to be unkind but she was also rather "dumpy". Some people are just born that way and Nancy was one of those people.

"Nancy," Smiff said. "Would it be a lot of trouble to make Mrs Mixly a cup of your best tea?"

"It would be a pleasure, Smiff," the girl smiled and glided silently out of the room like a good maidservant would. Nancy was a *pupil* at the Crime Academy, of course, but she used to be a maid to the Mayor of Wildpool, Sir Oswald Twistle, and she had loved her work . . . till the mayor and his wife had

thrown her on to the snow-covered streets.

Smiff went across to a tube that hung on the wall by the window. He pulled a cap off the end and blew down the tube. He placed the tube to his ear and, after a few moments, grinned, "We're in luck. Master Crook is in his office." The boy spoke down the tube and explained about Mrs Mixly. Then he put the tube back to his ear and listened, nodding.

Finally he pushed the cap back on the tube and turned back to the visitor. "Master Crook will see you now . . . ah, here's Nancy . . . let me take your cup of tea downstairs for you! But leave your handbag here."

"My handbag?"

"We have to be careful. Master Crook has enemies. We can't risk someone taking a weapon into the room and hurting him, can we?"

"I suppose not," she said and placed the bag on the table by the door.

The boy led the way to a door, opened it and went down some dimly lit steps. At the bottom was a small room with just a chair and a small table facing a curtain. Smiff left and as Mrs Mixly sipped at her tea a slight draught ruffled the curtain. A door had opened

43

behind it. There was a creak, as if a large man had sat down in a chair.

Master Crook's voice was deeper than the North Sea when the tide is in but warmer than the summer sands (when the tide is out, of course). "Good day, Mrs Mixly. How can I help?"

The woman took a deep breath. "I want you to teach my little twins how to make a life on the street. . . I did think they might make beggars, but the new police force would whip them and send them home. I thought your sign says you can do it without them being caught by the police?"

"Ah, the Wildpool police force . . . Constable Liddle and Constable Larch. Yes, stern upholders of the law. And, of course, their stout Inspector Beadle. But tell me, why would you want the poor children to beg? You are well dressed. You live in a large house and your husband has a good job in the shipping offices making ten shillings a week."

"How do you know all that?" the woman breathed.

"Master Crook's Academy has files . . . we study the town and its people. It's one of the jobs the

44

students have been doing since we opened. We don't
spend every day with classes and crimes, you know.
We gather facts and store them up. You never know
when you may need a good juicy fact," the warm
voice gurgled.

"Yes, my Albert has a good job . . . but all the
money goes to pay the bank for the money we
borrowed. The money to pay for a share in Lord
Fumble's railway," she said and pulled out a
handkerchief to dab at a sniffle.

*That happens, doesn't it? Writers say tears
run down when someone cries. But the truth is
snot runs down at the same time. They like to
say, "The woeful woman wept!" That is more
pleasant than saying, "The sad lady snotted."*

For the next ten minutes the story poured from
her as freely as her tears. She had held those tears
back when she spoke to her husband and the children.
But something about Master Crook's cosy room and
gentle voice made her rush and gush out her
troubles.

At the end Master Crook said softly, "I have heard

of other cases like this. There are many families who have suffered from Lord Fumble's little scheme."

"So you'll take the twins? You'll teach my Martin and Millie?"

There was a sigh from behind the curtain. "No."

"Ah!" Mrs Mixly cried. "But your sign promises. . ."

"Hush, my dear lady, and listen a moment. There are a hundred families in Wildpool alone who are in your sad scrape. The answer is not to send all the children on the streets to beg. That is not the Master Crook way. No, the answer is to deal with the problem. And the problem is Lord Fumble. Can you hold out just a week longer?"

"We've got by for two months now . . . though it was the poorest Christmas those children could ever wish to see."

"In a week I may have found a way to get your money back. One week."

The woman rose to her feet and began to climb the stairs. In the room above, the cap in the end of the speaking tube sounded a whistle. Smiff hurried across and listened. Then he dropped the tube, ran to a drawer in a cabinet, pulled out a purse and found two

golden sovereigns. He picked up Mrs Mixly's purse and dropped the coins in.

When the woman appeared at the doorway from Master Crook's cellar he was holding the open bag. "What are you doing?" she cried.

"Searching for a weapon," the boy said quickly. "It's a rule of the Academy. But there's no weapon there . . . oh, and we may be criminals but we don't steal from visitors!"

She shrugged. "I have nothing to steal."

Smiff gave a great laugh. "Hah! You have two gold pieces!"

"I haven't!" the woman argued.

Smiff pulled them from the bag, held them up to the light then dropped them back in. "You have now."

He handed the bag to Mrs Mixly. The woman wandered out into the February afternoon in a daze. "Apple pudding tonight for my little dears. Apple pudding . . . and custard!"

Back in the house Smiff grinned at Nancy and winked. Nancy's moon face glowed warm as the sun.

*

Helton Colliery – Wednesday, 15th February 1837

Helton Colliery sprawled like a black slug over a hill and a valley. Great grey mounds of slimy rock had been dumped on the earth like mini-mountains of waste. Huge wooden wheels on iron towers whirred and wound ropes that took men under the ground to carve the coal. Then they wound the other way to pull up trucks of rich and shining coal.

Steam pumps belched water from the workings into a rusty stream that had once been as clear as a tadpole's tail, but the poisoned tadpoles were long dead now.

Rattling belts carried the coal on overhead lines to railway trucks and filled them ready for the locomotives to carry them down to the docks at Wildpool.

Miserable men and grey-faced women trudged through the cold puddles; no one spoke and no one smiled.

"You could get a job here, old-timer," the farmhand said. "They're always looking for strong men."

Rick Turnip looked around the scene as bleak as the

dark side of the moon. "I have a job," he said proudly.

"What's that then?"

"I'm a highwayman . . . or I was before I spent a little time in Darlham Gaol. I robbed coaches. I'm from a long line of famous highwaymen!"

"Dick Turpin?"

"No . . . Rick Turnip."

The farmhand smirked and smothered a laugh. (They all did that.) "Well," he said, "you'll find the great people of the land hardly use carriages any more. They build railways and have their own railway carriages. Even stagecoaches are rare now."

Turnip climbed down from the cart and shook hands with the farmhand. "Thank you, my friend. I'll walk the rest of the way to Wildpool."

"Best of luck with the highway robbing – some of those rich people need to share it around a bit."

Rick Turnip nodded then turned his face to the cold north wind and followed the road that ran alongside the railway track. "Yes, I have a job," he said to himself. "Highwayman." There was a spring in his step as he left the ugly Helton valley behind and saw the smoking chimneys of Wildpool ahead.

To his right the sea was whipped white and green by the wind. Coal ships were coming and going up the river to dock at Wildpool quaysides and load up with the coal from the mines.

Locomotive No. 3 smoked and coughed its way up to the ridge. The trucks were empty but it was still quite a climb. A man stood in the doorway of a tiny hut by the track wearing a heavy black overcoat and carrying two flags, a red and a green. "Good afternoon!" he called to Rick Turnip as he passed him on the road.

"Good afternoon. Waiting for the train?"

"No. I'm a policeman," the man explained

"A law officer?"

"No, no, no! Not that sort of policeman. It's the name the railway companies give to track guards. Our job is to stop trains running into one another. We wave flags. Important job but not policemen like Constable Liddle and Constable Larch in Wildpool . . . they are part of the new police force. Very confusing, but don't worry. I can't arrest you! Hah!"

"Good," the ex-convict muttered and hurried down the hill towards the chuffing train. "What

can a highwayman do when there's no coaches and carriages to rob? Why, rob a train, of course!"

The railway policeman was out of sight. The old footpad felt a thrill of excitement as he took out his handkerchief, blew his nose then tied it round the bottom half of his face.

I wish he wouldn't do that. Why can't he have two handkerchiefs? One to blow his nose and one to wear as a mask. Blowing your nose on your mask is . . . well, it makes me a little sick to think about it.

He took a blanket from the bundle he was carrying and quickly threw it over his shoulder. "Just like Dick Turpin," he chuckled.

The footpad raised his fingers under the cloak so it looked as if he were carrying a pistol.

The pounding pistons of the train came closer. Rick Turnip stepped forward till he was almost touching the track. The mighty metal monster pulled level with him, engine roaring, pistons hissing, wheels clanking, steam spitting. Turnip had trouble hearing his own voice as he cried, "Stand and deliver, your money or

your life . . . ooooh! I do love saying that again!"

The driver stood on the platform behind the boiler.
His fireman shovelled coal into the firebox. They
heard nothing apart from their metal dragon's roar.
They saw an old man by the side of the track, wearing
a handkerchief and a blanket. The whooshing steam
blew the blanket away from Turnip's hand and left
him pointing a finger at the men on the locomotive.

The train roared on and the empty coal trucks
clattered past. The driver turned to his fireman. "Who
was that?"

"Dunno," the fireman said. "Probably one of those
trains-potters."

Chapter 4

GOLD AND GUARDS

Wildpool Town – Wednesday 15th February 1837

Now here's a strange thing . . . well, it seems strange to me. Maybe your life is so weird that nothing seems strange . . . not even a pink and purple parrot on your pillow. I don't know. But I found it strange that Master Crook set up his Crime Academy next door to the Wildpool Police Station.

Wildpool Town, and its mayor Sir Oswald Twistle, were extremely proud of their new police force in 1837.

There were three officers in that first year. In charge

was the mighty Police Inspector Beadle. His office was in the basement of the police station and some people believed he lived there. From time to time he came upstairs into the police station and when he did the stairs trembled as if an elephant was walking up them. In fact an *elephant* would tremble if it saw Police Inspector Beadle because the elephant would feel small.

Inspector Beadle

That February morning the stairs trembled.
The two constables, Liddle and Larch stood to
attention.

A maid polished the desk and a mop stood in
a bucket by the door. The whole place shone and
smelled of beeswax polish. The maid could see her
face in the shining desk top. It was a sharp face with
blue eyes like a doll and topped by curly fair
hair.

Beadle waddled in and stood behind his desk.
He sat in a chair that was as wide as a sofa. "Be seated,
men." He turned to the girl. "Alice . . . go and clean
the kitchen."

"Done it, sir."

"Then do it again. This is a private meeting with
secret matters to discuss. Go!" he said and the voice
was deep and menacing.

Alice went.

The constables dropped into two hard wooden
chairs. How can I describe these two fine law men to
you? I won't try. Here's what Police Inspector Beadle
wrote in his first report.

Liddle is thin, ancient and not very bright.

Larch is heavy, slow and as bright as a dark lantern.

Beadle passed them a sheet of paper.

WILDPOOL POLICE FORCE

Instructions

Date: 15 February 1837

PC Septimus Liddle (PC 01) and PC Archibald Larch (PC 02)
are hereby assigned to guard duty on the Wildpool and Helton
Railway Special Train. On Monday 27th February at 3:00 p.m.
the constables will report to Fumble Hall. A large quantity of gold
is to be loaded on to Lord Fumble's private carriage. Locomotive
No. 2 will divert from coal-hauling duties to pull this train. The train
will go to Wishington Country Manor where it will be unloaded.
Constable Liddle and Larch will not let the Fumble Fortune
Carriage out of their sight until the money is safely stored in the
safe at the Manor.

Police Inspector Beadle

Constable Larch asked, "But who will guard Wildpool while we are rushing off on train duty?"

Police Inspector Beadle nodded, "I shall."

Constable Liddle frowned. "Are we supposed to work for private persons . . . I mean Lord Fumble can hire his own bodyguards."

"He could . . . but the mayor promised Lord Fumble that the mighty Wildpool police would take on this task. It is a large amount on money and the future of Wildpool Railway depends on it. And the future of Wildpool depends on the railway. The railways are spreading across the land like roots from a mighty tree. Every town that is connected to it will grow. Every town that is not connected will wither and die."

"I see," Liddle said . . . though he didn't.

Larch smiled happily. "I always wanted to ride on one of those train things. I've heard Lord Fumble's carriage is like a room in his house . . . seats covered in velvet, cabinets full of wine and a stove to warm it and to make him nice hot tea."

"You will be riding in the guard van behind," Inspector Beadle sighed. "It's more like a room in

Darlham Gaol . . . wooden benches, no wine and very cold. But the Wildpool police force are happy to suffer a little discomfort for the honour of guarding the Fumble Fortune."

"Are we?" Liddle asked, a little miserable.

"We are," Beadle said. He slapped his massive hands on the desk and pushed himself to his feet. "But over the next week we have to work at the road safety campaign we talked about last week."

"Oh, sir, do we have to?" Larch groaned. "I got a terrible battering yesterday."

"It was your own fault," Liddle smirked. "The road safety campaign says you have to help old ladies to cross the road, keeping them safe from horses, carriages and carts."

"I did that! I got Dame Winter all the way across without even a splash of mud."

"Yes," Liddle reminded him, "but Old Dame Winter didn't *want* to cross the road, did she?"

"No," Larch sighed. "She battered me with her umbrella."

Beadle simply shook his large head and left the room to go back to his office in the basement.

"Come on then, Larch," Liddle said tucking his instructions into his notebook. "Let's go and help children across the road from Dame Winter's School. At least the children don't batter you with umbrellas."

"But one of them gave me a nasty bite on the kneecap last week!" Larch argued as he followed Liddle out of the room . . . leaving his copy of the instructions on the wooden chair.

Silence. *Click!* The door opened. Alice slipped into the room. She saw the paper on the seat and picked it up. She read it. She smiled. The girl folded it and ran across to the door. She took a dark cape from a peg to keep out the February wind then hurried out of the door into the street.

Evening dark came early in Wildpool winter and the lamp-lighter was wandering down the streets turning on the gas-green glow to brighten the smoky streets.

"Evening all!" Liddle and Larch called as they passed him.

Alice White didn't go very far. She made sure Constables Liddle and Larch had plodded around the

corner then she turned into a gateway of the building next door – the one marked with a red sign that said, "Master Crook's Crime Academy".

An old man was standing at the front door talking to the boy Smiff. Smiff saw Alice coming up the path, tugged the old man inside and said, "Hello, Alice. What's new?"

She waved the police report in front of him. "This! Wait till Master Crook sees this!" She smiled at the old man. "Hello. You must be one of the new teachers Mr Dreep told us about."

"No . . . I . . . er . . . who's Mr Dreep?"

"Our teacher . . . Master Crook's assistant." Alice lowered her voice and muttered, "Some of us think Mr Dreep may be Master Crook just pretending to be Mr Dreep and that Master Crook isn't himself except when he's pretending to be himself. See?"

"No."

"That way, if we ever get caught and the police try to arrest Master Crook, we can always say we have never seen Master Crook . . . which none of us has, unless Mr Dreep is really Master Crook in which

case we *have* seen him but we can't swear in court we've seen him because we didn't know we were seeing him when we saw him if you see what I mean?"

"No . . ."

"It all makes perfect sense," she shrugged.

And of course it DOES make perfect sense, doesn't it? Especially if you're a person potty enough to have a pink and purple parrot on your pillow. If it doesn't make sense then I have just one thing to say to you . . . Ask your parrot to explain.

"So what are you going to teach us?" she asked eagerly. "NOT that I'm in school at the moment, of course. I'm working next door as a maid and really I'm a—"

"Alice!" Smiff cried. "This gentleman is a stranger. We know nothing about him. You can't go blabbing our secrets to a stranger."

"Who says? You says?" she asked angrily. Alice turned to the stranger. "You look like a criminal to me," she said.

"Do I? Why thank you, young lady. I come from a great criminal family . . . a family of highwaymen!"

"Here!" Alice cried. "I *told* you he was our new teacher! Mr Dreep said our next big crime would be highway robbery, didn't he? Well?"

"He did," Smiff nodded.

"But . . ."

"Alice will take you to Mr Dreep."

"Who says? You says?" Alice exploded. "Take him yourself. I'm off to see Master Crook. I have some *very* important business with him." She walked across the room and blew down the message tube.

Smiff shrugged his skinny shoulders. "Come into the kitchen. Mr Dreep's making us some supper. Want some?"

He led the way out of the classroom and down the corridor to a warm room where a fire glowed. Kettles and pots hung from the mantel-shelf and some bubbled and spat over the fire with the rich taste of best beef soup.

A tall man stirred the pot. He smiled as Smiff entered. The man had a fine, white smile under a

thin, dark moustache. He would have been handsome but for his eyes that bulged just a little like pale gooseberries. His shirt was as fine and white as his smile and the sleeves were rolled up as he worked.

"Good evening, my friend. Can I help you to some soup? You look as if you could do with a good meal."

"I've lived on bread and water for forty years," the old man said.

"You'll eat well here, never fear. We look after our teachers like lords," Dreep said. He wiped his hands on a towel and stretched out his right hand to shake the old man's. "Samuel Dreep at your service. And you are?"

"Rick Turnip, sir."

"From the famous Turnip family of highway robbers? What an honour to meet you, sir! Why, children still sing songs of your famous Tom Turnip as they skip and play ball games," Dreep laughed. He pulled a book from a shelf. "Here's a collection of street rhymes . . . look!"

Tommy Turnip

Tommy Turnip caused alarm
Bandit robber with one arm.
Wildpool called him nasty curses
Cos he nicked the women's purses

Tommy Turnip roamed the streets
Stealing little children's sweets
Tommy Turnip, law men got 'em
When he pinched a lady's bottom

Tommy Turnip came to harm, he
Got caught pinching someone's sarnie
Tommy threw his arm away,
Lived to rob another day.

Tommy Turnip is no good
Chop him up for fire wood
If the fire won't burn his head
Use his wooden arm instead.

Dreep shook the old man's hand. "And of course *you* are just as famous!"

"I am?"

"Oh, yes. Master Crook still talks about the great wrong that Lord Fumble did to you. What was it? Forty years in prison?"

"Yes, sir, forty years," the old man sighed. "But they weren't too bad. In fact I had some happy times," he added. "The best bit was showing the new criminals the ropes!"

"The hangman's ropes?" Smiff gasped.

"No . . . it's a saying. Showing someone the ropes – teaching them how to get along in the prison. I miss that," he said softly.

Dreep rubbed his thin, white hands. "But now you are here you have a whole future of teaching our students about highway robbery. Master Crook will be so pleased to see you."

"Well, that's the thing, sir," Rick Turnip said. "I didn't come here to *teach* . . . I came here to *learn*. Lord Fumble caught me when I tried to rob his carriage all those years ago. These days they have railway engines instead of coaches. I haven't a clue how to rob one of those things! I tried earlier today. I ended up looking a real prawn."

Dreep stirred the soup and began to spoon it out into a bowl. He placed it on the table with fresh, crusty bread he'd baked earlier in the day. "Mr Turnip, you rob a train in the same way you rob a carriage."

"How?" the old man asked, sniffing at the soup and dipping in a piece of bread.

"You're the greatest highwayman Wildpool has ever seen. YOU tell ME!" Dreep said.

Turnip sucked on the bread and let the soup warm him from the inside as the fire warmed him on the outside. In Darlham Gaol he had forgotten what warm was. "First, you have to stop it," he said.

"Exactly!" Dreep clapped.

"But I don't know how to stop a railway engine," the old convict moaned.

"Neither do *I*," Smiff said. "But at Master Crook's Crime Academy it's our job to find out."

"I see," the old man said, his heart growing warm at the thought that he was among friends.

"And THEN you need to find a train worth robbing," Dreep said.

"Stop it, rob it, job done."

"I will look at the business of stopping a moving train," Dreep said.

"And Master Crook will tell us when and where there will be a train worth robbing!" Smiff finished.

"How will he do that?" Rick Turnip asked.

"He has his ways," Smiff said wisely.

As the fearless three were in the kitchen plotting, Alice was in the cellar below passing a paper through the curtain to Master Crook.

There was a long pause with just the soft rustle of paper. Finally Master Crook's low voice said, "You have done well, young Alice. Now take the paper back to where you found it – if they think their plan has been stolen the police will suspect you and sack you. They will also change their plan."

"That's good thinking that is!" Alice chuckled.

"We have just one week to work out how to rob a train."

"I've heard of *highway* robbery but never a *train* robbery," Alice said.

"Then the students of Master Crook could be about

to pull off the world's *first* train robbery!"

"Great," Alice said. "I like the sound of that."

"And one last thing," Master Crook crooned softly. "Give Nancy a message. She will meet the old man who's just arrived, his name is Turnip. I do not want her to tell him her name – her family name. Understand? And hurry."

"What *is* her name? Why shouldn't she tell him?"

Suddenly the Master's voice grew loud enough to make the curtain tremble. "You ask too many questions, Alice White. Do as I say or you'll be back on the streets selling matches."

Alice glared at the curtain. "Who say? You says?" she said. But she said it very, very quietly.

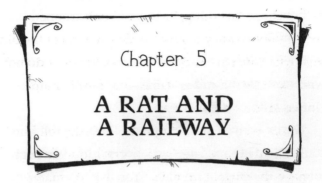

Chapter 5

A RAT AND
A RAILWAY

Wildpool Town – Wednesday 15th February 1837

Nancy showed Rick Turnip to a large, airy room on the upper floor of the Crime Academy. "Here you are, Mr Turnip. Your bedroom."

The old man looked around, worried. The wide windows looked out over Wildpool. It was a clear night and a three-quarter moon glowed in the frosty sky. The school stood on the road overlooking the river. Bright lights shone in the shipyards where men worked through the night to build ships. Gas street-lamps sparkled over the frost-dusted cobbles.

A few carts skidded along the roads, shivering men and women hurried towards the taverns. Stray dogs

sniffed for rats in the dark alleys. Stray cats watched from the tops of black-brick walls. The rich rode warm in their carriages to the theatre, wrapped in fat furs.

"I'm not used to this," the old man said.

"I've made up a lovely comfortable bed for you with fresh sheets and warm blankets. The mattress is stuffed with goose-feathers."

The ex-convict shook his head. "I don't think I could sleep in that," he said. "Sorry, but I've spent forty years sleeping on a board with just a blanket. No lights and just the sound of men moaning."

Nancy nodded. "Why not sleep on the floor then," the chubby girl said kindly. "I'll pull the curtains so the light doesn't come in. Sorry I can't do the moaning men."

"You're a good girl. What's your name?"

"Nancy, sir."

"Nancy what?"

The girl turned even paler than usual. "I'm not supposed . . . I mean . . . I'm just Nancy, sir."

"Thank you, Just Nancy!" the old man smiled. "It's not my old cell in prison, but I'm sure I'll be happy here."

Nancy bobbed a clumsy curtsey, the way she used

to do when she was a maid to the mayor. She took the candle and closed the door, leaving the old man in darkness.

Wildpool Town – Thursday 16th February 1837

The next morning the students at Master Crook's Crime Academy sat at the tables in the teaching room. They had maps and sketches of the Wildpool and Helton Railway as well as blank paper and pencils to make notes. Samuel Dreep stood at the front of the class with Rick Turnip and rubbed his thin hands together.

Alice, Smiff and Nancy looked at their teachers eagerly.

Yes, this is a really weird thing. Children who ENJOY school! Since 1870 children have been FORCED to go to school. You are probably one of them, poor thing. Rick Turnip had forty years locked away all day, just as you school pupils are . . . but at least no one forced him to listen to a boring old teacher droning like a bee and stinging with his cane like a wasp. Schools? They're a crime. But NOT Master Crook's.

"Students, may I first welcome the famous, the infamous, the incredible Mr Rick Turnip!" Samuel Dreep cried. The class cheered and clapped while the old convict blushed. "This great highwayman robbed the rich single-handed."

"Erm," Rick interrupted. "I think you are thinking of Tom Turnip . . . he was single-handed cos he only had one arm."

For a moment Dreep was flustered. "Quite . . . yes . . . as I was saying . . . this man robbed Lord Fumble without any help from anyone. And now, forty years later, he is going to do it again!"

Cheers.

"Am I?" Turnip asked.

"Why, yes. The train we are planning to rob is Lord Fumble's train with Lord Fumble's fortune on board. This was the man who had you locked away for forty years!"

Smiff jumped to his feet. "Revenge time!"

"Oh, I'm not interested in revenge," the old highwayman sighed.

Smiff sat down suddenly. But Nancy jumped to her feet. "You're right, Mr Turnip. This is not about you

and Fumble. This is about saving the families Fumble cheated. Saving them from starving! This is about people like the Mixly family. This isn't revenge . . . it is justice!"

The girl raised a fist above her head. Smiff and Alice looked at her in silent awe.

"Thank you, Nancy," Dreep said with a faint smile on his face. "I can see you have taken Master Crook's ideas into your heart." Nancy sat down. Dreep turned to Alice and took a deep breath.

The sort of deep breath you would take just before you stepped into a cage with a man-eating lion . . . or even a woman-and-child-eating lion. You take a deep breath for courage. And what do you get? Courage? No, you get air.

"What you did yesterday with the police note was wonderful work. . ."

Alice glowed with pride then felt Mr Dreep was going to say "but. . ."

"But," he said carefully. "We need you back inside the police station. You are our eyes and ears in that place. The more you can learn about the enemy the easier it'll be to defeat them."

"Awwww!" the girl groaned. "I wanted to do the robbery!"

"I know you did, Alice, but we each have a job to do and spying is your job."

Alice stuck out her bottom lip and decided to be awkward for the rest of the lesson . . . which she was.

The Mixly twins were excited.

"Daddy! Daddy!" they cried.

Mrs Mixly slapped a hand on the breakfast table. "Really, Martin and Millie, you must not make a fuss at the breakfast table! It is bad for your father's stomach. He must eat his food in peace."

"But . . ." Millie moaned.

"I said NO, Millie Mixly, and that means No." She placed a pie in the middle of the table.

The twins sat in silence supping their porridge as their father carved into the pie and tucked into it hungrily. "It's a long time since we had any meat in our meals, Mrs Mixly," he said happily. "Where did you say this pigeon came from?"

"The cat brought it in, Mr Mixly," she said.

"And jolly tasty it is too," he said, mopping the gravy with a morsel of bread.

"But—" Martin began.

His mother raised an eyebrow and he fell silent.

Mr Mixly wiped his mouth on a napkin then rose to his feet. "Time I was off to the bank. I'll work all the better with that pigeon pie inside me."

"That's what I thought," his wife said.

The man put on his tail coat and top hat then wrapped a scarf around his neck to keep out the Wildpool winter wind. He picked up a leather case full of papers and went to the front door. "I'll be working till midnight to make some extra money," he said.

"Again?" Mrs Mixly said, shaking her head. "You're a good man."

"And I have a good wife, feeding me like that." He stopped and smiled down at the children. "Now, you two rascals, what were you trying to tell me?"

Millie looked at Martin. Martin looked at Millie. "We were going to tell you, the cat brought in a fat pigeon," the girl said.

"I think I know!" their father cried smacking his lips. "Be good. See you tomorrow." He stepped out

of the door and strode up the street.

Mrs Mixly frowned. "Your father will have *proper* food tonight. I can go shopping with the money I found after my visit to Master Crook's Crime Academy. No more pigeons that the cat dragged in."

Martin looked at Millie. "It was a funny-looking pigeon that the cat caught," the boy mumbled. "It looked like a very fat rat to me."

Millie gave him a bright smile. "If Father wants to think it was a pigeon then let him," she said. "Better that way."

Martin nodded. "Much better."

"Now, class," Dreep was saying to the Crime Academy class. "Mr Turnip has already told us the first part of any highway robbery is to stop the carriage. That was easy with the old horse-drawn coaches. You just scared the driver into stopping the horses," the teacher explained and pointed to a picture on the blackboard.

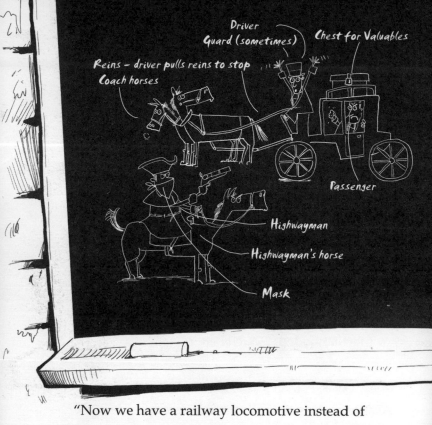

Driver
Guard (sometimes)
Chest for Valuables
Reins – driver pulls reins to stop
Coach horses
Passenger
Highwayman
Highwayman's horse
Mask

"Now we have a railway locomotive instead of
horses. These things travel at up to forty miles an hour.
They are past you before you can blink," Dreep went
on.

"As I found out yesterday," Turnip tutted.

"The driver even has a wind shield he can hide
behind if a robber pointed a gun," Dreep went on and
showed another picture.

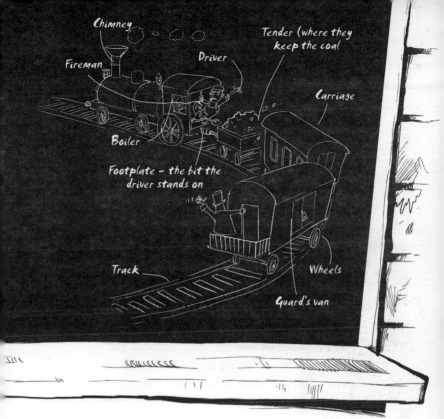

Chimney

Fireman

Driver

Tender (where they keep the coal

Carriage

Boiler

Footplate – the bit the driver stands on

Track

Wheels

Guard's van

"No one can stop *that*!" Alice snorted . . . being awkward and unhelpful.

A slow smile spread over the face of the old highwayman. "Ah, but you are wrong, young Alice. Someone *can* stop it."

"Who says? You says?"

"The *driver* can stop it!" the old man said quietly.

"Oh, yeah, well, of *course*, I know *that*!" she said

angrily. "But none of us is driving the treasure train, are we?"

"Why not?" Smiff said suddenly. "Mr Turnip is a genius! We always knew he was. One of us drives the train and stops it in a quiet spot."

"Hah!" Alice sneered. "Not only can you not drive a train, master smarty Smiffy, but they wouldn't *let* you. Caw, I've eaten pork pies with more brains than you got."

This is gruesome but true-some. Pork butchers in Wildpool were not too fussy about what they put in their pies. If they slipped in a little pig brain then no one would notice once it was cooked. Pies are checked carefully these days. But they just don't taste as good as they used to, do they? Someone isn't using their brain.

"And I've seen pork pies that are prettier than your face," Smiff said, rising to his feet.

"You won't be eating pork pies, Smiff, you'll be swallowing your teeth if you don't watch it!" she raged.

"Who says? You says?" the boy laughed.

"Here! You can't say that! *I* say that!" Alice roared and Nancy had to grip her wrists to stop her lashing out at Smiff.

Dreep looked on and did nothing to stop the fight. "Smiff can be very irritating, can't he, Alice?"

"You're telling me. I wish I didn't have to share a room with the little mongrel," she snapped.

"But you *don't*, Alice!" Dreep explained.

"Don't I?"

"No! You can go back to the street corner selling matches in the ice and snow. You can sleep in that burnt out house by the shipyards the way you used to. You can scavenge in shop bins for scraps of food like you used to. You don't have to stay here and suffer with Smiff. The door is over there – close it behind you." He spoke softly but his gooseberry-green eyes were as cold as the North Sea.

Alice sat down. "I will stay. But not for simple Smiff. It's like we said before. We are doing this for the Mixly family." Her thin mouth shut like a mousetrap. End of argument.

"Now, where were we?" Dreep asked, smiling again. "Mr Turnip said the driver can stop the engine.

So we have one week to train him as an engine driver."

"Me? No one would give a job to *me*. I'm fresh out of Darlham Gaol and I have the Turnip name," the old man objected.

"No, your name is Urnip and you worked as a coach driver for Lord Fumble. Now that his coaches are idle he wants you to learn how to become an engine driver," Dreep said. Then he added an awful joke.

. . . one that I am almost ashamed to repeat, it is so bad.

"He wants you to re-train! Ha! Ha!"

No one laughed (can you blame them?).

"He's right, though," Alice said. "No one will give him a job."

"They will if Lord Fumble *orders* it," Dreep said. "And I have here a letter from Lord Fumble doing just that!" The teacher placed a sheet of writing paper on the desk and the students bent their heads to read it.

THE FUMBLE ESTATES

The Manager
Wildpool and Helton Railway Company
Wildpool Station
Station Road
Wildpool
16 February 1837

Dear Sir

This letter is to introduce Richard Urnip to you. The man has served as a coach driver on Lord Fumble's Darlham Estates for forty years. He is the most reliable and hard-working person ever to have been in our employ. However, now the carriage work is reduced. His lordship does not want to dismiss such a loyal servant. He wants Urnip to be taught how to drive a steam locomotive on the Wildpool and Helton Railway.

There will be a special train that will run from Fumble Hall to Wishington Country Manor on Monday 27 February 1837. His lordship would be pleased if Urnip could drive the locomotive that day.

Yours faithfully

Andrew Brown – Estate Manager

The class were amazed at the letter. "Where did you get this, Mr Dreep?" Smiff asked.

The teacher shrugged. "I have friends in the Wildpool world of crime. I know my share of forgers and they produced this for me."

"It's perfect," Smiff said.

"It's all right I suppose," Alice grumbled.

Nancy cleared her throat and said softly, "We have a problem. . ."

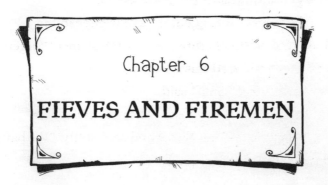

Chapter 6

FIEVES AND FIREMEN

Fumble Hall — Thursday 16th February 1837

Lord Jeremiah Fumble, 16th Lord of the Fumble family, sat in the topmost tower of Fumble Hall. Downstairs the floors were marble, the ceilings covered with gold leaf and from the walls hung portraits of all the great Fumbles in history. After forty years as a judge he was losing count of the men, women and children he had sent to foul fates. That was a sadness. He liked to remember every one of the fearful faces, the sobs of shock and the fainting fits that his savage sentences brought on. On winter nights the memories warmed him like glowing coals.

"The Fumbles came across with William the Conqueror," Lord Fumble used to boast. "Sir Giles de

Fumble was such a great warrior he was rewarded with these lands at Wildpool."

The lands at Wildpool were owned by the Saxons. William the Conqueror could not "give" the lands to anyone. The Normans just "stole" the land and battered anyone who tried to argue. The Fumble family were fieves . . . sorry, thieves. In 1837 the last Lord Fumble was the biggest thief of them all.

BORN 1040 IN ROUEN.
KNIGHTED IN 1066 AD
ON THE BATTLEFIELD
AT HASTINGS BY KING
WILLIAM I OF ENGLAND
AND NORMANDY.
KILLED 10 SAXONS IN
BLOODY BATTLE WITH HIS
OWN BLOODY BATTLEAXE.
MARRIED LADY MATILDA
DE PARIS (WHO WAS NOT
A BATTLEAXE).
BECAME MASTER OF THE
WILDPOOL ESTATES IN 1067.
HAD 58 REBELS BURNED
TO DEATH IN WILDPOOL
SAXON CHURCH 1068.
DIED 1106 – POISONED
BY MATILDA DE PARIS.
SURVIVED BY SON – GILES
THE JOLLY.

Visitors to Fumble Hall were shown around the gloomy pictures of gloomy, glaring men with horses, and gloomy men without horses.

There were some gloomy pictures of horses without gloomy men . . . but even the horses looked gloomy. No wonder Lord Fumble wanted to escape Fumble Hall. What is the word I need to describe the place? Gloomy, perhaps?

Fumble Hall had once been a castle to keep out the poor people who hated the family . . . and there were lots of those. Over the years the lords had fitted warming windows and cosy curtains, draught-proof doors, comfy carpets and soft seats that sat in front of coaly fires.

But Lord Jeremiah did not like the place. The scruffy little town of Wildpool was spreading and new houses were pushing up to the walls of the Fumble Hall Estate. The coal mines on his land made him a fortune but they were filthy and fouled the air with smoke and choking dust.

"I want a new house in the country," he had told his estate manager, Andrew Brown, three years ago. "Near enough to my mines and my money . . . but away from these *common* people. Wishington Country Manor is old – I want to knock it down and build a fine new Wishington Country Manor. But I need money. A million pounds should do it."

Brown spread his hands. "The railway is the coming thing, my lord," Brown said. "That's the way to make a million." He was a grey and grinning ghoul of a man. His hands twisted around one another like slippery snakes.

"Can I afford to build a railway? I don't want to risk my money. It's taken me years to squeeze my million pounds from the peasants in the fields and the miners in the mines. Do you realize ninety of the foolish men died last year when Helton South exploded? Have you any idea how much that cost?"

"Ninety lives, perhaps?" Brown said in his slithery voice.

"It cost me thousands of pounds. We had no coal for a week while they dug out the corpses. Why, I even paid the widows of the dead men. I gave them the wages their husbands would have earned in a week. A whole week!"

"And then threw them out of their cottages, my lord, to bring in new miners," Brown reminded him.

"Brown!" Lord Fumble fumed. "I did *not* throw them out. They are my cottages. Since their men no longer worked in *my* mines I asked them to find

somewhere else to live."

"And if they had nowhere?"

His lordship stabbed a fat finger at his manager. "There are workhouses, Brown. Workhouses for the poor who are too idle to work."

"Yes, my lord," Brown bowed and writhed. "Some are too old or sick to work," he said quietly. "They need your help." Lord Fumble paced the room and ignored his pitiful plea.

"So how do I build a railway? I don't want to risk the Fumble fortune!"

"Sell 'shares', my lord. Sell a thousand shares at a thousand pounds a time and you will have a million pounds. A railway will serve your mines and cost just a hundred thousand pounds or so. Promise the shareholders that it will link up with the main lines and, when the railway is making money, they will make a fortune . . . a hundred pounds a year at least. They can live on the hundred pounds a year . . . or they can sell their share for *two* thousand pounds!"

"Are there enough stupid and greedy people to fall for that?"

"Oh, yes, my lord. The world is full of stupid and

greedy people . . ." then he pulled out a handkerchief to wipe his wet lips and muttered, "You only have to look into a mirror to see one."

And, let's face it, Andrew Brown could have looked in the mirror and seen a greedy man. Make no mistake, some of Lord Fumble's million found its way into the Brown pockets. When it comes to money you can't trust anyone.

That had been three years ago. Now the new Wishington Country Manor had been built and it was time to move.

As I said, Lord Jeremiah Fumble, 16th Lord of the Fumble family, sat in the topmost tower of old Fumble Hall. It was not a fine room but it was the safest place to store gold. There was only one stairway up to the top room and three doors, each opened with different keys.

The gold glowed in the light of a lantern. It was polished gold, worn smooth by Fumble fingers. Each coin was loved by the lord. Each coin was placed in one of two oak chests that were bound with iron bands and locked with unbreakable locks.

"I'll see you again when we get to our new home in Wishington Country Manor. Farewell, my lovelies!"

Master Crook's Crime Academy — Thursday
16th February 1837

In the classroom of Master Crook's Crime Academy,
quiet Nancy had shocked the class by speaking out so
boldly. "We have a problem," Nancy had said.

"I learn to make a locomotive go," Rick Turnip said.
"I learn to make it stop. No problem."

"You aren't alone on the footplate," Nancy said.
"There is a fireman there with you. The man that keeps
the fires going. All sorts of things could go wrong."

"Go on," Samuel Dreep urged her.

"The fireman could try to stop you and you could
get hurt. The fireman could share the blame and
be hanged . . . even though it wasn't his fault. The
fireman may have to flee for his life and leave his wife
and children to the workhouse."

"So what's the answer, Nancy?" Alice asked.

"We need a fireman on the footplate as well as
Mr Turnip as the driver. Someone from the school."

Smiff jumped to his feet. "I can do that!"

Dreep stroked his chin with his long fingers.
"Put some coal on the fire, Smiff, while I think

92

this through," he said.

Smiff walked across to the fireplace, took a shovel and pushed it into the coal. "No!" the teacher cried. "Pick up the whole bucket and throw some coal on to the fire."

Smiff shrugged. He reached out for the handle of the large coal scuttle. He tugged. It barely moved from the hearth. He heaved, it rose about the thickness of a toad's toe and then he had to drop it. He tumbled backwards.

Nancy rose and crossed to him. "Let me help," she said. She picked up the bucket easily and scattered coal on the fire.

"I think we have found our fireman," Dreep said.

"But. . ." Smiff began to object.

"Nancy has been carrying coal buckets up and down stairs at the mayor's house for years. She's the strongest person in the room."

"Yeah . . . but a fireman can't be a firewoman!" Smiff grumbled.

"We'll cut her hair and send her with Mr Turnip as a boy . . . his grandson, shall we?"

Smiff blew out his cheeks. He was fed up, but saw the sense.

And so it was agreed.

The plan took a long time to make but at last Dreep had it written down.

The great Wildpool Train Robbery

MONDAY 20TH FEB

Rick Turnip and Nancy present themselves at Wildpool Engine Works as trainee driver and fireman. (Nancy will have had her hair cut by the way.)

TUESDAY 21ST FEB

2:00 p.m. Smiff and Samuel Dreep will take a hay wagon from the Crime Academy and drive it to the spot where the Great North Road crosses the Wildpool line to Wishington Country Manor.
(This will be a test run for Monday.)

WEDNESDAY 22ND FEB

8:00 a.m. Rick Turnip and Nancy start work on the Helton Colliery coal train.

SUNDAY 26TH FEB

Day off. Some students may wish to go to church.
Some (no names mentioned, Alice) may need to go more than others.

MONDAY 27TH FEB

8:00 a.m. Rick Turnip and Nancy drive the Helton Colliery coal train. They take locomotive No. 2.

2:00 p.m. Smiff and Samuel Dreep will take a hay wagon from the Crime Academy and drive it to the spot where the Great North Road crosses the Wildpool line to Wishington Country Manor.

(Allow 1 hour and 30 minutes for journey. We will check the timing later.)

3:00 p.m. Locomotive No. 2 travels to Fumble Hall where a carriage full of gold will be waiting.

3:10 p.m. Nancy will pretend to check the couplings and will unfasten Lord Fumble's carriage and the Guard's Van with the police officers on board.

3:15 p.m. Locomotive No. 2 will travel west out of Fumble Hall. It will be driven to the spot where the Great North Road crosses the Wildpool line to Wishington Country Manor.

(Allow 30 minutes for journey.)

3:45 p.m. Locomotive No. 2 will arrive at the crossing with the Great North Road. Gold transferred to wagon and hidden under hay. Rick Turnip and Nancy abandon train. All return to Crime Academy.

TUESDAY 28TH FEB

6:00 p.m. Meeting of shareholders of Helton and Wildpool Railway. £1,000,000 given back to shareholders.

7:00 p.m. BIG CRIME ACADEMY PARTY. ANOTHER JOB WELL DONE.

Mister Dreep pinned the plan on the classroom noticeboard.

"Perfect," he said. "Nothing can go wrong. Nothing."

Oh, dear. Oh, dear. Oh-dear-oh-dear-oh-DEAR. What happens when someone says that?

Darlham Gaol – Thursday 16th February 1837

In Darlham Gaol a boy was led in through the great green gates. The prison officer took the chains off his wrists and off his legs.

The governor of the prison stepped out of his office to meet the newcomer.

The little boy's lip trembled like a swallow's wing and tears flowed down his dirty cheeks.

"Alexander Adams, sir," he said wearily. "Found guilty by Justice Fumble in Wildpool. Sentenced to three months in the gaol for picking a gentleman's pocket and stealing a silk handkerchief."

"Still as harsh as ever after all these years," the governor chuckled. He wrapped an arm around the trembling boy's shoulders. "Been to gaol before, Adams?"

The boy shook his head and tears splashed on the

stone paving. "No . . . sir . . . I only . . . only took it to keep Mum out of the workhouse. Dad has all our money tied up in the railway shares."

"I understand," the governor said. "We have a few more like you. So dry your eyes! We have an old gentleman in here who looks after new lads like you!"

"Do you sir?" the boy asked, drying his eyes.

"Yes! The famous old highwayman, Rick Turnip."

"I've heard of him," the boy gasped. "And he'll look after me?"

"Yea . . . er . . . oh, dear me . . . no! I forgot . . . he's not with us any more! Oh no! What shall I *do* without him?"

"Never mind *you*!" the boy wailed. "What am *I* going to do without him."

His pitiful sobs would have melted a heart of the coldest Darlham Gaol stone.

A tragic thought, eh? Melting a heart of stone. Except I have never in fact met anyone with a heart made of Darlham Gaol stone. Not even Lord Fumble. His heart was the same squidgy and blood-filled sack that we all have. But never mind. Imagine it.

Chapter 7

BOILERS AND BAILIFFS

Wildpool Engine Works – Wednesday 22nd February 1837

The driver of Locomotive No. 2 was in a rage. He was dressed in his green, corduroy suit and black cap. He was a man of wire in the body and fire in the brain. His badge said, "William Rump".

He glared at Rick Turnip and Nancy (who was now dressed as a boy, you will remember.)

You DON'T remember? Oh, come along. Keep up. She has to pretend she is a boy to get a job as a fireman on the railway. Picture her with her hair cropped and a coarse, woollen suit on.

Then he glared at the letter for the third time. It had the crest of the Fumble estates at the top and the signature of Andrew Brown at the bottom. It ordered the railway company to give Richard Urnip a job AND give him the task of driving the treasure train.

"Do you know what it takes to become an engine driver?"

"Well . . . I've driven coaches for thirty years. . ."

"Aha!" the driver screeched like one of his rusty truck wheels. "It says here *forty* years!"

"Does it?" Turnip muttered miserably.

Nancy put in quickly, "But you were a footman on the coach for ten years before that . . . that's what Mr Brown should have said."

William Rump the driver turned purple with rage. His eyes bulged as they strained to burst out of his head. "Exactly! Ex-ACT-ly! You have to spend years . . . *years* . . . before you have the right to be a driver. Years. You start as a cleaner. Getting up before daybreak and crawling under the engine and over the engine and inside the cab, scouring and cleaning and greasing and brushing till you are blacker than the coal in that tender." Rump jerked his thumb at

the tender full of coal behind him.

"But this is urgent," Nancy said softly.

The driver ignored her and raged on, "Then you become a 'Passed Cleaner' – that means you can light the fire in the firebox so it's up to steam when we start . . . that takes about ten years and THEN you can become a fireman. And after ten years as a fireman you can become a driver and after ten years as a driver . . ."

"You'll probably be too old to see where you're going," Rick Turnip muttered.

". . . you become a main line driver."

"On the Helton and Wildpool railway? You can only go ten miles in any direction . . . it's not what you'd call *main* line, is it?" the highwayman argued.

"So, you want to get thirty years' work into three days? Is that right?" Driver Rump sneered.

"It's an *emergency*," Nancy said with a quiet smile. "There are only two drivers for the two Wildpool and Helton locomotives . . . and you have to have a day off, don't you? I mean. You work harder than anyone I've ever met," she added. "You deserve a day off."

The driver sniffed. "I do. But his lordship

could bring in proper drivers from other railway companies," he grumbled.

Turnip shook his old head slowly. "They wouldn't come. He pays the meanest wages in the railway world."

Rump nodded, glum.

"And," Nancy added, "he buys the cheapest steam locomotives. They are so badly made they are dangerous."

Rump suddenly lost the wire in his body and his head fell forward. "Locomotive No. 1 exploded," he nodded. "The driver, Johnny, was like a brother to me. And the fireman was a lad with a wife and two children. Terrible."

"They buried them in Wildpool," Nancy said, holding the driver's trembling arm. "I remember there was a big funeral in the town. The mayor gave a speech. I heard him practising."

"You did?"

"I was his maid," Nancy said then snapped her mouth shut and wished she could snap back the words.

"His what?"

"Ahem. . ." she choked. "I . . . I was his . . .

maid's . . . brother! No! I mean I *am* his maid's brother," she managed to say.

The driver nodded. "It was a good speech," he said. "I remember Mayor Twistle's speech. He said the drivers were the heroes of the modern age . . . explorers at the frontiers of the world."

Nancy said, "Mayor Twistle said the driver and the fireman did not die in vain!"

"No. They died in bits," the driver sighed. "In fact . . . between you and me . . . there were not a lot of bits in those coffins. They were scattered a fair way round Wildpool and Helton. What they didn't find I guess the dogs and the foxes must have eaten by now."

Nancy felt a little sick at the thought.

I hope you don't. It's not as if someone asked you to pick up the pieces. Now THAT would make most people sick. But in all the horrific railway accidents someone has to do it. I wonder who?

Driver Rump gave another deep sigh then turned to the Crime Academy pair. "Sorry . . . you're right. We

need all the help we can get. If I'm bitter about Lord Fumble and his mean ways, I shouldn't take it out on you two, should I?"

"I understand," Nancy said.

The driver rubbed his hands together. "Then let's get started. You, lad . . . what's your name?"

"Nan— Norman," Nancy said.

"Right, Norman. The driver may turn the knobs and push the levers and turn the wheels . . ."

"And get the most shillings," Nancy said.

"That as well . . . but it is the *fireman* that makes the fire that heats the water that makes the steam. Not only is it a hot and sweaty job but it is also the one that needs the most skill. You don't just throw coal into the firebox!"

"No?"

"Oh, no! You have to scatter it in just the right way and in just the right amount. Too much and you make black smoke and sparks. Too little and the ash falls through the grate. Too hot and the steam just blows away through the valves – too cool and your locomotive can't pull the bonnet off a baby."

"I've spent five years keeping the mayor's fire

going. . ." Nancy began, then remembered to keep her lips sealed.

For the next hour she learned all about firebars and smoke tubes, brick arches and firebeds, the difference between Bedwas coal and Durham coal and how to check if the fire is burning just right.

The fireman has to see that the smoke is light grey . . . not too dark and not too light, but just right. A bit like Goldilocks and her porridge . . . except you don't see the Three Bears driving a train.

The fire was built up till it was perfect and Driver Rump turned to the controls. "I move this lever to make the train go faster or slower," he said.

Nancy turned to Rick Turnip. "That's the regulator," she said.

"How do you know that?" Rump exclaimed.

"I read some books about steam locomotives before we came here," she said. "Was that all right?"

Rump blinked. "Very admirable, young man. Very. I like the cut of your jib."

This is something sailors usually say. But of course the railways had only been running a dozen years or so in 1837. Who knows what Driver Rump had done before he joined the railway company? A mole catcher perhaps?

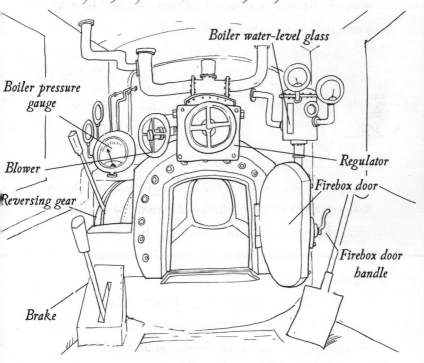

Boiler water-level glass

Boiler pressure gauge

Blower

Reversing gear

Regulator

Firebox door

Brake

Firebox door handle

By the end of the day they had made two trips to Helton Colliery and carried two loads down to the coal drops at the river edge.

By the time the two Crime Academy companions reached home that evening it was dark and it took them two baths each to get clean.

"Well?" Samuel Dreep asked as they walked through the door of Master Crook's Crime Academy.

"So much to learn," Rick Turnip sighed.

Nancy smiled. "But Mr Turnip is so clever we'll be ready to drive solo by the end of the week. Don't worry. He's a genius."

The old man blushed. "I've been called a few things in my time . . . but never a genius," he chuckled and settled into a chair.

Wildpool Town – Thursday 23rd February 1837

There was a knock at the door while Mrs Mixly was feeding her children cabbage soup for dinner. She had picked up the leaves from the market cobbles when the stalls had shut down for the night. The two gold coins were kept to buy food for their father.

"Who's that at the door?" she asked.

Millie and Martin looked at one another. "I hope it's not a thief!" Martin cried and wrapped his arms around the cabbage soup to save it from a soup-snatcher.

Millie spooned her warm, green water quickly into her mouth till it dribbled down her chin.

Mrs Mixly opened the door a crack and saw two young men there. They were tall and almost as wide as the door. Their muscles had muscles and their clothes were as black as the Helton coal. They wore shining top hats and smiles as cunning as cats.

"Mrs Mixly?" the first one asked. "I'm Candy."

"Then my children would love to eat you!" she giggled.

Mrs Mixly didn't giggle because she thought her joke was funny. She giggled because she saw two handsome young men and she "came over all silly", as they say. Who says "came over all silly"? Well, I do for a start.

"And I'm Knuckle," the second one said.

"That's *handy*," the woman said and this time she giggled like a hen because she was sure that was the funniest thing anyone had ever said.

Knuckle blew out his lips in a bored way. "I've never heard that one before."

"Really?" Mrs Mixly smiled. "Not everyone's as witty

as me . . . or as pretty as me," she added, trying to flirt.

Candy didn't flirt. "We have been sent by the Northern Brick Bank," he said.

"Oh! They loaned us the money to buy this house!" the woman cried. "How odd that you should call. How lovely to meet you. Come in and take a chair."

"We've come to take them all," Knuckle said. An empty cart stood outside, waiting.

"I don't understand," Mrs Mixly said and her flirty smile was fading as Candy pushed his powerful shoulder against the door and barged into the hall. Mrs Mixly backed into the living room and sat down heavily at her seat at the table.

"Your husband is Maximus Mixly," Knuckle said and he ground the knuckle of his hand into the palm of the other hand.

"Sorry," the woman fluttered. "He's still at work. He works extra hours to make the money to pay for the railway share. Look, there it is above the mantelpiece!" she said proudly.

The two men didn't look. "The thing is, Mrs Mixly, you borrowed money and the bank wants it back. You owe a hundred pounds."

"And the bank shall *have* it back as soon as the railway starts to pay its way and we are rich," she said.

Candy leaned forward till his beery breath was in her face. "The thing is, Mrs Mixly, the bank can't wait for ever. It wants its money *now*."

"But we don't have it," she shrugged.

"Then we will take every stick of furniture and sell it and give the money to the bank. We will take every pot and kitchen pan," Knuckle said.

"Every stitch of clothing, boots and shoes and pictures from the walls," Candy added. "We will sell them and give the money to the bank," he explained.

"And then, if that's not enough, and if you haven't paid the money by the end of the month the bank will take your house," Knuckle chuckled.

To have a bully chuckle at your misery is a terrible thing. But, worst of all, is a Knuckle chuckle.

"Where will they take our house to?" Millie asked.

Knuckle pulled a pained face. "I *mean* we will *sell* your

house to someone who can afford to pay."

Martin stood up and looked the bully straight in the belt buckle . . .

Aha! You are waiting for me to say it was a "Knuckle buckle" aren't you? Well, I'm not going to. That would be a pitiful joke and I do not do pitiful.

"If you take our chairs where will we sit?" the boy asked boldly.

"On the floor," Candy answered.

"If you take our beds then where will we sleep?" Mille asked.

"On the floor."

"And if you sell our house, where would we go?" Mrs Mixly gasped.

"Out the door. Not our problem, lady," Candy said. "We are bailiffs. We are only doing our job."

"Throwing a woman and her helpless children out into the cold, cold snow?" Mrs Mixly wailed.

Candy looked at Knuckle. "It's not snowing, is it, Knuckle?"

"Not when we came in," his partner replied. "But

don't worry about that now, Mrs Mixly. You have a week to find the money." Knuckle leaned closer to her and hissed, "There is a very good trade in skinny children to sell to chimney sweeps. We could get twenty pounds each for your brats! For now we'll just take the furniture." He lifted the chair, with the woman sitting on it, and carried it as if it was as light as a wren's feather . . .

and you don't get any feathers lighter than a wren's.

Mrs Mixley jumped to the floor and fell to her knees. She clung to the leg of the man as he walked to the door. "Please, I beg you on my knees!"

"It's *my* knees you're on," he snarled and kicked her away.

Five minutes later the house was empty. There wasn't even a candle left to warm the little family. All that was left was the railway share in its frame on the mantelpiece. "Please, oh, please don't take that!" Mrs Mixly moaned.

Knuckle looked at Candy and Candy looked at

Knuckle. Knuckle looked at the pitiful family sitting in the faint light of the half-moon that shone through the window. "Why would we want to take a Helton and Wildpool Railway share? They are ten a penny – in fact, they aren't even worth the paper they're printed on. The bank would laugh if we took that back with us."

"Only a mug would pay a thousand pounds for that," Candy spat.

"My husband Maximus did," Mrs Mixly sobbed.

"Then he was robbed," Knuckle said. "Robbed."

The men turned and opened the door, letting in the chill wind off the Wildpool river. "Sleep well," they said.

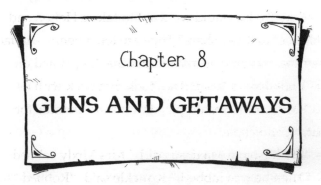

Chapter 8

GUNS AND GETAWAYS

Fumble Hall — Sunday 26th February 1837

The door to Fumble Hall was wide and white. It was meant to look smart and modern but the old building still looked like a crumbling castle . . . with a posh white door instead of a drawbridge. A handle on a rope hung at the side. Police Constable Larch reached up and pulled it.

Deep inside the huge house a bell jangled.

After an age the door was opened by a man dressed as a butler with a black tail coat, grey trousers, white shirt and white cravat tie. "You rang?"

"I am Constable Liddle and this is Constable Larch. We've come to—"

"Back door!" the butler hissed. "Servants must use the back door."

"I'll have you know we are officers of the law and—" Liddle began but he was speaking to a white door that had been slammed in his face.

"Back door it is," Larch shrugged. His red face was redder than ever and his piggy eyes were more piggy than a pig's. In fact they were so piggy a pig would be ashamed to have eyes like that.

They tramped along the overgrown path, through clumps of cold, damp grass, round the side of the Hall till they reached the green kitchen door.

Larch said, "Leave this to me," and knocked firmly.

The door opened and a man stood there dressed in country clothes – green tweed suit and high riding boots. "Yes?" he asked. "What do you want?"

Larch's mouth moved but no words came out. Just sounds at first. "*Splutter . . . splitter . . . splatter . . . butter . . . but . . .*" then, "But . . . you're the *butler* who answered the front door!"

"So? I can't wait all day to answer doors, you know. Lord Fumble wants his money's worth. I am a butler when the front door bell rings, I am his estate manager

114

when business calls. My name is Andrew Brown. And
you are. . ."

"I told you at the front door," Liddle said. He
was as thin as a chair leg, with a moustache that was
whiter than the front door of Fumble Hall.

"You told the *butler*," Brown argued. "I am no
longer the butler. Do I look like a butler?"

"No, but. . ."

"Then tell me your names and your business,"
Brown ordered.

*Aha! you cry. This is the man who was with
Lord Fumble just a chapter or two ago. Why is
the humble Fumble servant suddenly Brown the
bully? Because some people are like that. They
crawl to the powerful but boss the less-posh. There
is a name for people like that. The name is "creep".*

"We carry your truncheons like flaming torches
of justice. Bring light to the darkness of our savage
streets," Larch said proudly.

"Yes, yes, yes . . . flaming truncheons are all very
well. Nice and warm on a day like today. Just be
careful you don't set fire to the curtains. But what I

mean is, what are you doing here today?"

"We have come to talk about the guard job we're doing tomorrow," Liddle said.

"Guarding the Fumble Fortune!" Larch said in an awed voice. "Over a million pounds, they say!"

Andrew Brown twisted his pale hands together. "A dangerous job! If any of the Wildpool villains knew about this they would cut your throat as soon as look at you. They would all want to get their hands on this fortune!"

"Cut our throats?" Liddle choked.

"As soon as look at us?" Larch squawked.

"And your flaming truncheons would do you no good at all," Brown added. "What you need are some real weapons!"

"Real weapons?" the policemen chimed together like the front and back door bells.

"And we have them here in Fumble Hall," Brown smiled.

"Suits of armour?" Liddle asked.

"That would keep the knives out," Larch breathed.

"Swords and shields and crossbows and battleaxes . . . a flaming battleaxe would be better than

a flaming truncheon, Larch," Liddle said.

"Not sure I could use a sword, a shield, a crossbow and a flaming battleaxe," Larch complained. "I haven't got enough hands."

"I see what you mean. . ." Liddle began.

"No!" Brown cried. "Not the old weapons. I meant the new weapons. Lord Fumble likes to go shooting grouse and pheasants. . ."

"That's against the law!" Liddle gasped. "He can't go round shooting his farm workers! Can he?"

"Pheasants, Liddle, not peasants," Larch explained.

"Lord Fumble has some fine shotguns," Brown went on. "No villain with a knife will come near you if you were each carrying a shotgun." He led the way into the main hall of Fumble Hall, over the cold stone floor, past the glowering pictures of the long-gone Fumbles, past the lances and shields, the heads of dead deer and wild boar, the great iron candle-holders with their dead and shrunken candles. It was gloomy. No wonder Lord Fumble wanted to move out. There were tapestries on some of the walls, faded and grey and torn. They seemed to be showing men murdering animals in hunting scenes from long ago.

Brown pushed a tapestry aside and showed them through the heavy door that stood behind. "Here we are, officers, the Gun Room."

All sorts of guns hung on the walls. There were flintlocks and matchlocks, arquebusses and musketoons, coach guns, calivers and carbines, toradors and tanegashimas, petronels and fowling pieces.

"Most of these are just for show," Andrew Brown explained and pointed to an arquebus.

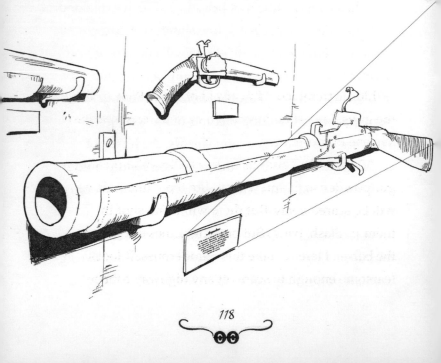

Arquebus

The match is clamped in a clip called the serpentine. Squeezing the trigger forces the serpentine downward, and brings the burning match in touch with the priming powder resulting in a spurt of fire flashing through the touchhole and igniting the main charge inside the barrel.

Liddle trembled. "I'm afraid of guns. Well . . . not the guns. I'm afraid to guard a train if Constable Larch has one of those things."

"Quite right," Brown said. "I will fill them with gunpowder so, if you have to fire them, the villains will be scared away. But there will be no shot in them. . . Flash, bang! But nothing comes out of the barrel. Here . . . take this blunderbuss. It looks fearsome enough to scare off any highway robber."

He took down another gun from the wall.

Blunderbuss

Dutch "thunder-tube". 1700. Firing lead balls. Barrel 40 to 60cm. Useful for defending mail coaches, guarding prisoners or street fighting and popular with pirates. A flared muzzle to make loading easy and to scatter the shot around. When the trigger is pulled, a spring action causes the striker to strike the flint, showering sparks onto the gunpowder in the priming pan; this fires the main charge in the barrel, propelling the shot.

"It scares me," Larch agreed.

Brown smiled. "Many years ago . . . about forty years I think . . . a highwayman tried to hold up Lord Fumble's coach with a finger hidden under his cloak."

"Where did he get the finger from?" Larch gasped. "Did he cut it off one of his victims?"

Brown shook his head. "Turnip, was the name."

"He cut the finger off a turnip? I didn't know turnips had fingers!"

Brown's mouth twisted madly. "Just take a gun each and get out before I have to shoot Constable Larch. Now," bossy Brown said, "let's look at the line and the carriages you'll be guarding." He led the way out through the kitchen door and across the garden to a long shed at the edge of a field.

A railway line led into the shed. Brown pulled open the shed doors and there stood three carriages. They were painted a bright shade of yellow and even in the dim winter light of the shed they glowed. The Fumble crest decorated the sides.

"First class!" Liddle said. "The poor people have to travel in carriages with no roofs and hard wooden seats. I bet he has satin cushions!"

121

They climbed aboard the first carriage.

"No satin cushions," Larch said.

"No seat!" Liddle said.

"This is the goods carriage. We'll use this to move all the valuables from Fumble Hall to Wishington Country Manor later on. But tomorrow this will be the carriage we'll use to load the treasure."

The estate manager led the way to the back of the carriage. He opened a door, crossed the link and opened the door into the next carriage. This one smelled of fine leather and rich wine. The yellow silk seats were soft enough to lose a cat in. "Lord Fumble's carriage," Brown said.

"Ohhhh! We'll be very comfortable in here," Liddle said.

Brown sneered, "You won't be IN here . . . you'll be in the guard's van behind."

He led the way into a small brown truck with bare wooden walls and rough wooden shelves that would serve as seats. Liddle and Larch sat carefully on one.

"Comfy enough," Larch said. His seat was padded by his fat bottom.

"Hard as stone," Liddle said. His bony backside felt every splinter of wood on the solid seat.

"It's less than ten miles," Brown said. "Half an hour." He spread out a plan on the small table in the centre of the van.

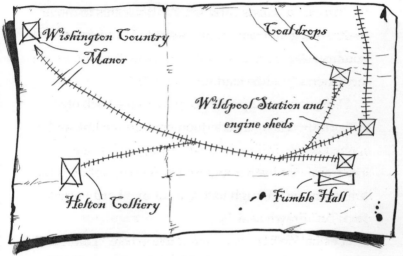

Liddle and Larch nodded.

"The locomotive will arrive at two p.m. after its second coal run of the day. It will reverse down the branch line to Fumble Hall here and collect these carriages. It will then head west to Wishington Country Manor."

Brown waved a fine, pale finger over the plan. He tapped a spot on the map. "Here is where the railway crosses the Great North Road. If I were a robber then *that* is where I would stop the train."

"Why?" Liddle asked.

"Because you have to get the gold off the train, on to a wagon and away. You need to stop the train near a road. That, gentlemen, is where we will need you with your guns!"

"Ooooh!" Liddle sighed.

"I think I need a pee!" Larch said as he shivered with the thought of meeting some hideous highwayman.

The train with the empty coal trucks struggled up the hill to Helton. "We haven't enough power, Nancy," Rick Turnip sighed as he pushed the regulator as hard over as he could.

Nancy nodded. "I know. That's the tricky bit about being a fireman. You can't make too much steam or it's wasted. But you can't make too little or we run out . . . like we have now."

The locomotive spluttered and spat and the cranks clattered slower and slo-wer and sl-ooo-www-errr.

"So what's the answer? It's no good running out of steam tomorrow if the police are chasing us!"

"The answer is to learn the line," Nancy explained.

"If I know the hills are coming up then I can get just the right amount of steam. When we do this run again this afternoon I'll be better."

"But we're not doing this run tomorrow. Tomorrow we're going to Wishington Country Manor," the old man pointed out.

Nancy nodded. "So, we finish the second run but instead of going back to Wildpool engine shed we tell the railway policeman to turn the points toward Wishington Country Manor!"

"Will he do that?"

"Wave the Fumble family paper under his nose and he will," the girl smiled.

Turnip nodded. "It'll be getting dark by then, but you're right. You know, Nancy, you have a great criminal brain."

"But I'll never be as famous as you," she said and began to sing softly as she shovelled coal and built up the steam again.

"Tommy Turnip is no good
Chop him up for fire wood
If the fire won't burn his head
Use his wooden arm instead."

Rick Turnip was right. By the time they'd finished their coal run the sun was setting, blood red, behind ragged silver clouds. They pulled away from Wildpool Coal Drops over the river where the coal ships waited.

They reached the line from Wildpool to the west. The railway policeman said, "Not going back to the sheds for the night?"

"No," Nancy sighed. "Lord Fumble wants us to move some furniture from Fumble Hall to the new Wishington Country Manor."

The railway policeman heaved the lever to set them on the track to the Hall. "I hope he's paying you overtime," he said.

"Not a chance," Rick Turnip grumbled.

"You'll be the last train out tonight so I'll leave the points set so you go straight back to the sheds," the railway policeman promised and waved them goodnight.

The locomotive headed west towards the dying light. They passed the Fumble Hall branch; Nancy changed the points so they could back down the line towards the Hall. They arrived in the dark parkland and shuddered to a halt just before their wagons

bumped into the shed with the yellow carriages.

"Right," Nancy said. "Let's do a trial run to Wishington Country Manor." She turned over the Fumble letter which was grubby by now and as they moved forward she marked how many minutes there were between the climbs and the falls and how steep they all were.

After half an hour they came to the Great North Road. Turnip gave a long blast of the steam whistle and cows by the roadside ran for their lives.

"How long to unload the gold?" Nancy asked.

"Five minutes," the highwayman said.

"So I have five minutes to build up the steam for a fast getaway," Nancy said and marked the spot on the map.

"No, no!" Turnip cried. "Once we empty the Fumble Fortune at the road here we abandon the train. That's the plan!"

"But if we leave it here then Inspector Beadle's policemen will find it all the quicker."

"They can't run after a train!" the highwayman said with a frown.

"No . . . but if they think quickly they could saddle

up one of his lordship's horses. They would catch up soon after we stopped here. If I take the train on to the end of the line they'll follow the train, not your slow wagon. You'll have much more time to get away!"

"But what about you?" the highwayman asked.

"I can jump off as the train runs out of steam near the Country Manor and walk back to the Crime Academy. We'll meet up there."

"I don't like you taking that risk," Turnip moaned.

"I'll be all right," Nancy said. "I'll be fine."

Oh, dear. Master Crook is a Master Crook. If he makes a plan you have to stick to it. Start making changes to the plan and you are heading for trouble. I can just see it coming . . . as one cow on the railway line said to the other. But it was the last thing that cow ever said. Know what I mean?

As the sun had set over Fumble Hall there had been a light in the topmost tower room. Lord Fumble had been stroking his precious chests of gold. "I love you so much, my lovelies, I think I will have you buried with me. We can't have you falling into the hands of the poor, can we? They'd only spend you on food. Such a waste that would be."

The shuffling sound of the locomotive made him move to the window and look out over the gardens to the railway shed.

He watched as a line of empty coal trucks shunted down the line to his private platform. The train stopped. Fire flared in the locomotive cab, the fire door closed and the train set off again.

"Curious," Lord Fumble mumbled. "I must remember to mention this to Brown."

Brown was down in the dining room, dressed as a butler and ready to serve dinner. "Nothing to worry about, my lord," he said and began to wring his hands. "The engine crew must be practising. I believe they are new men . . . replacing the ones that were . . . err . . . blown apart."

"That will be it," Lord Fumble nodded.

But as Brown walked to the kitchen he said quietly, "Curious. I must forget to mention this to Inspector Beadle!"

Chapter 9

SECRETS AND
A SHOVEL

Monday 27th February 1837

Nancy was a bright girl. She soon learned the skill of
being a fireman, and what a skill it is! We all remember
12 June 1899 and Armagh. That date is burned in the
memories of railway men and women.

Nancy got it right. She sweated and puffed as
much as Locomotive No. 2 but still found time to look
out of the cab and wave at the trains-potters by the
roadside.

Rick Turnip and Nancy drank large mugs of tea at
Helton Colliery while they waited for their coal trucks
to be filled.

"It's a good life," the old man sighed. "If I hadn't

ARMAGH TRAIN TRAGEDY: 80 DEAD, 250 INJURED

LOCOMOTIVE FAILS ON STEEP, 3-MILE CLIMB

The train had no brakes and ran back down the hill.

Carriages smashed into the train that was running behind.

Many victims were children, out on a jolly day trip. The fireman got it wrong.

gone to Darlham Gaol I could have been an engine driver." He took out a grubby handkerchief and wiped away a tear or two.

"Are you crying for your wasted years in gaol?" the girl asked.

"No . . . I'm crying cos I miss my old life in the prison cell . . . the library . . . all the friends I made."

Nancy stroked his arm. "You have friends in the Crime Academy. And you're enjoying this, aren't you?"

The highwayman tried to give her a cheerful smile through his soot-stained face. "I suppose so. I did so much *good* at Darlham though. I helped all the frightened new prisoners settle in."

"You're doing good if you steal the Fumble Fortune," Nancy said. "There are people starving in the streets because that loathsome lord tricked them out of their money." She remembered seeing a cart-load of the Mixlys' furniture as it rolled past the windows of the Crime Academy.

Alice had sighed, "Some other poor soul has lost their furniture. They'll lose their house next and be out on the streets like I was. In winter too."

"They could be moving house," Nancy had tried to argue.

Alice had looked at her with pity. "Not when the

cart's being led by Candy and Knuckle. They're the bank bailiffs. That's probably some other poor victim of the Fumble fraud."

Rick Turnip gave a sharp nod. He put down his empty tea mug. "You're right, lass. Let's fill up our water tank and we'll be on our way!"

"One more trip here then we're ready for the first great train robbery! You'll be as famous as Tom Turnip . . . *more* famous!" she laughed.

At two p.m. Samuel Dreep stepped out of the Crime Academy on to the path that led to the front door.

A cart stood there. The piebald horse was held by two men as wide as Locomotive No. 2. "Good afternoon, Mr Candy, good afternoon, Mr Knuckle," the teacher said.

"Afternoon," the two men grunted. Smiff stood a little way behind him and glared at them. He knew how these two men made their money.

"Thank you for hiring me your cart," Dreep said and stroked his fine moustache.

"Half a crown, you said," Candy reminded him.

The teacher took some silver from his pocket.

133

"Half a crown *each* is what it's worth to me," Dreep said. "After all, you could be losing business. You could be out there tearing toys from some child's little hands, or bottles from babies, or washing from women or squeezing money from men or cribbing coins from the blind beggar on the corner of the High Street!"

"You what?"

"I said, you do a wonderful job for the bank. Thanks to brave lads like you the poorhouse is full of families, the banks are crammed with cash and the Fumble Fortune is fatter than you!"

Knuckle nodded. "That's true, sir. Where would the world be without people like us? Where?"

"It has been a pleasure doing business with you, gentlemen," Dreep said smiling, but his grin was grim. "Now, Smiff, time to collect a little hay and then it's off to the Great North Road."

I know, Master Crook could have hired a cart from lots of places. He just liked the idea of using the bank bullies' wagon to carry away the cash. He was a strange man was Master Crook.

*

At three p.m., Locomotive No. 2 had dropped its second load of coal and was headed west on the line.

When they reached the branch to Fumble Hall the railway policeman gave Rick Turnip a cheerful wave. "Afternoon, Mr Urnip. Off to the Hall?"

"That's right. Special job. This job is so secret there are only two people in the world who know what we'll be carrying – me and Lord Fumble."

"Ooooh! Yes! You have to be careful! If any villains found out you was carrying the Fumble Fortune they'd be all over you like wasps round a jam pot!" the man said as he pushed the points lever to send them on the track towards the Hall.

"That's right," Turnip agreed. "Only you, me and Lord Fumble know about the treasure."

"And me," Nancy put in.

"Yes," the highwayman nodded, "only you, me, Norman here and Lord Fumble know about the treasure."

"Exactly what the estate manager Mr Brown said last night!" the railway policeman agreed.

Turnip sighed. "Only you, me, Norman, Mr Brown

and Lord Fumble know!"

"That's what I told the lads in the tavern last night!"

"Thank you and good afternoon," the highwayman snapped.

"Right. See you in half an hour," the railway policeman said with a wave.

Turnip backed the locomotive down the branch to the Fumble Hall shed. "It seems so many people know about this trip we'll be lucky if we aren't robbed fifty times before we meet with Mr Dreep. The secret of being a good highwayman is . . . well . . . to know a secret. But, if everyone knows, then it isn't a secret any more! Steady with the steam there, Nancy, we'll probably have to wait a while for them to load the treasure."

Nancy rested on her shovel and looked over the tender towards the carriage shed. "No. Mr Brown is waiting. Those policemen, Liddle and Larch look as if they're loading the treasure coach already."

"All the better. The less time we spend there the better. You know what to do?"

"Yes," Nancy said and her heart was flapping in her

chest like a sparrow in a greenhouse trying to get out.

The train slowed to a halt and gently bumped against the treasure carriage. Nancy jumped down, climbed under the tender of Locomotive No. 2 and fastened the coupling to the carriage. She then hurried along the side of the track.

"Where are you going?" Constable Liddle asked. He waved an ugly gun towards her.

"To check that the carriages are all coupled safely," Nancy said. She held up her hands that were black with coal and grease. "I don't mind if you do it!" she offered.

Liddle stepped back. "No! No, lad. You carry on!"

"I thought you might say that," the girl murmured and went to the coupling between the treasure coach and his lordship's travelling carriage. She shook the linking chain. It was tight. These carriages were hardly ever separate. They had been joined for three years and were stuck fast.

Nancy ran to the cab of the locomotive, grabbed her shovel and ran back. She used the shovel to hammer at the link and shake the rust free. Lord Fumble heaved

his heavy body out of his carriage. "What's all the noise?"

"Sorry, sir," Nancy said. She looked up at the fat face of the lord and the man stared back at her.

"Don't I know you from somewhere?" he asked.

"No, sir," she said.

"I never forget a face!" he argued and stared harder. "I have seen you before."

"I . . . er . . . used to work for Mayor Twistle," she remembered. "You were sometimes a guest at the house."

"And you?"

"I was . . . a footman!"

"You're a bit small to be a footman," the lord snapped.

"That'll be why you remember her!" Andrew Brown said helpfully.

"No, Brown . . . I remember her from a long time ago . . . thirty or forty years ago." He stroked his chin and climbed back into his carriage to have a glass of port and try to remember.

Nancy's hands were shaking so much she almost

missed the link with the next swing of her shovel but it caught and the link fell loose.

"Only Master Crook and Mr Dreep know my secret," she moaned as she lifted the heavy chain off the hook. "I hope we get away before Lord Fumble remembers!"

Alice huddled in her warm woollen coat, gloves and scarf. Since being at Master Crook's Crime Academy she didn't shiver in the whistling winter winds any more. Now Master Crook made sure she was warm and well fed.

She knocked at the door and the knock sounded hollow – like tapping on an empty box.

The woman who answered the door had two children clinging to her skirts. Their eyes were hollow and hopeless with hunger. "If you've come to take the furniture away you're too late. There isn't any left."

Alice swallowed tears. "No," she said. "No . . . I came to deliver a leaflet." She checked the list Master Crook had given here. "Mrs Mixly?"

"Yes."

"Read this . . ."

139

THE SHAREHOLDER
WILDPOOL AND HELTON RAILWAY COMPANY
27 FEBRUARY 1837

DEAR SIR OR MADAM
THIS LETTER IS TO INFORM YOU THAT LORD FUMBLE WILL
BE PAYING A DIVIDEND TO ALL SHAREHOLDERS OF THE
HELTON AND WILDPOOL RAILWAY.
PLEASE PRESENT YOURSELF TO THE APOLLO MUSIC HALL,
WILDPOOL, SOLE LESSEE – MR FARLAND   AT 6 P.M. ON
TUESDAY 28 FEBRUARY 1837.
IMPORTANT. DO NOT FORGET TO BRING YOUR SHARE
CERTIFICATE WITH YOU. NO PAYMENT WITHOUT A
CERTIFICATE.
YOURS FAITHFULLY,

Andrew Brown – ESTATE MANAGER

"Money?" Mrs Mixly sighed.

"Food?" the Mixly twins cried.

"Yes! Tomorrow night you'll have food!" the

woman said, crushing the letter in her excitement. "Oh, your dear father always said Lord Fumble was a great man and he'd repay us one day."

"But what will we eat the food off, Ma?" Millie Mixly asked. "We've no table, no plates, no knives, no forks, no spoons."

"We'll buy some," the woman sobbed. "We'll buy some."

Little Millie coughed weakly and slipped to the bare wooden floor. "Ahhhh!" she said and fainted.

Alice caught the girl. Alice wasn't much taller than the Mixly twin but little Millie was just a cotton dress full of bones. The Crime Academy pupil spoke quickly. "No need to wait for tomorrow to eat, though. We've plenty of food up at my school . . . most of the students are out rob . . . er . . . on a school trip. I've got thick soup and fresh bread, fresh fried fish from the market and creamy custards."

"Ooooh!" Mrs Mixly swooned at the thought.

"No! Don't you go fainting too!" Alice cried. "I can't carry you all up the hill. Come on, follow me. We'll have you fed from your toes to your head in no time."

141

The Mixlys followed Alice on to the street.

Alice walked quickly and remembered the argument she'd had that lunch time with Master Crook in the dark basement. "How come Smiff and Nancy get the exciting job – robbing a train. And you give ME the boring old job of taking leaflets round the houses. I'm not some blooming serving maid like Nancy, you know."

Master Crook had given a deep sigh. "Alice, we are like pieces on a chessboard – we all have different jobs to do. But we are working to the same end – to defeat Fumble's wicked plan. Smiff and Nancy get the excitement but *you*, Alice . . . *you* get the joy of bringing happiness to Fumble's victims."

"Who says? You says?" she'd barked back.

Now, as she opened the door into the Crime Academy kitchen, and saw the tear-stained faces of the marvelling Mixlys, she mumbled, "Yeah, all right, Master Crook, you was right."

It was 3:15 and the plan was running on time. Nancy ran to the cab of Locomotive No. 2 and began to feed the firebox with just the right amount of coal for the

142

climb out of Fumble Hall fields.

Rick Turnip watched the steam gauge as the needle swung higher. He had to get away on full power and as quickly as possible. When the gauge was past the mark, the fire roaring, the steam screaming to escape and the boiler bubbling he reached for the regulator.

In the guard's van at the back Constable Liddle suddenly said, "I think one of us ought to sit with the treasure, just in case something goes wrong! Inspector Beadle told us not to let it out of our sight."

Larch argued, "No. He told us not to let that treasure carriage out of our sight. Nothing will go wrong! The estate manager has it all planned. We are just here for the ride. I've never ridden a steam train before. I'm going to enjoy it. I've got a bottle of beer and a cheese sandwich. You go if you want but I'm staying here!"

When he said "I'm staying here," he meant he was staying in the guard's van. He didn't mean "I'm staying here . . . in the guard's van at Fumble Hall carriage shed." But we know that's EXACTLY where he would be.

The tall, thin constable stepped from the guard's van and walked towards the front of the train. He walked past Lord Fumble's carriage and reached the treasure carriage.

At that moment Rick Turnip pushed the regulator. Locomotive No. 2 jumped forward like a stone from a catapult.

There was a crash as the coupling to the treasure carriage went tight. "Here! Don't go without me!" Constable Liddle cried . . . though no one could hear him in the clattering roar of the moving engine. He struggled to pull the door open but it was too stiff. He looked back to see if he could climb aboard Lord Fumble's coach and saw it wasn't moving.

Constable Liddle wasn't as bright as one of his buttons but even he saw what was happening. "Stop that train!" he cried. As the back of the treasure coach rattled past him he grabbed at one of the flag ropes that was fastened to the back of the yellow coach. He dropped the gun. It struck the iron rail and exploded. It had no bullets in but it did have a cloth backed in to keep the powder in. The burning cloth struck the seat

of Liddle's trousers and the wind whipped it into a flame.

His arms ached as he was lifted off his feet. His shining boots sparked and skidded off the platform and he was towed along like a smoking kite on a steam-driven string. "Ooooh! Me bum's on fire!" he wailed but there was no one to hear him.

"We've done it," Nancy cried. "We've escaped with the loot!"

But, oh, Nancy, what's that burning blue thing with silver buttons flapping behind?

If this was the first great train robbery, then Constable Liddle was the first policeman in the flying squad! His skinny legs flew out behind him like twigs . . . so he was also the first policeman in Special Branch. . .

Twigs . . . Special Branch, geddit? Oh, never mind.

145

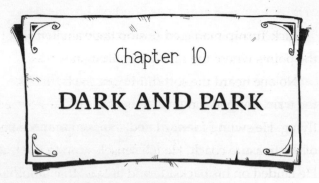

Chapter 10

DARK AND PARK

3:30 p.m. Monday 27th February 1837

Nancy worked steadily and had the fire glowing perfectly. Locomotive No. 2 climbed away from Fumble Hall steadily, happy to have a coach with treasure rather than a long line of heavy coal trucks.

They reached the main line in ten minutes and slowed to a halt. Without a guard's van it was tricky because the guard's van had the brakes.

Yes, I know that to us modern folk of 1901 a train without brakes is a shocking thing. But true! Drivers just turned off the regulator and let the locomotive drift to a halt. If they wanted a really

quick stop they would throw the reverse lever.
Dangerous and deadly . . . but so is cholera.

Rick Turnip managed to stop the train just short of
the points where the railway policeman waited.

No one heard the soft thud from the back. As
the train stopped moving Constable Liddle stopped
flying. He swung forward and smacked into the back
of the treasure coach. He fell senseless on to the track.
He landed on his backside and at least that smothered
the fire in his pants.

"Let us through to the main line," Turnip called.

"Can't do that," the railway policeman said. "The
last coal train of the day is on the line, coming the
other way. You'll have to wait till it's passed."

"How long?" Nancy asked, anxious. She looked
back towards Fumble Hall. No one was coming . . .
yet. But a fast horse could catch them in ten minutes.

"Ten minutes," the railway policeman said.

Nancy groaned and went about keeping the fire in the
box an even glow. She had plenty of coal but it was a while
since they'd taken on water. If the boiler ran dry then it
could explode . . . just as Locomotive No. 1 had done.

Rick Turnip tapped his hands on the regulator. Nancy chewed her nails and that left her with black lips. Lord Fumble and the policemen had been left behind but if there were horses in Fumble Hall stables they could catch them if they waited much longer.

After twelve minutes the coal train from Helton huffed past. The driver of Locomotive No. 3, Driver Rump, gave Turnip a cheery wave. Then the coal-train driver looked ahead and gave a scream.

A figure in a navy uniform and a battered top hat was staggering towards the track in front of him. He threw the engine into reverse and it slowed but not quickly enough. Constable Liddle walked into the side of the cab and bounced back on to the cold ground beside the track.

Nancy watched the coal train in horror and saw the dazed policeman fall. He fell face down and she could see Liddle's scorched buttocks smiling up at the sky. At least the coal train had cleared the points. She cried to the railway policeman, "Let us through . . . in the name of Lord Fumble . . . let us through!"

The man threw the points, Turnip pushed the regulator and Locomotive No. 2 jumped forward

on to the main line and headed towards Wishington Country Manor.

Driver Rump on Locomotive No. 3 climbed down and knelt beside the battered Constable Liddle. "What are you doing? Trying to kill yourself?"

Liddle shook his head. "Stop! Thief!" he croaked.

Rump pulled the stopper from his water flask and poured some into Liddle's bleeding mouth which had stained his wisp of white moustache red. The thin policeman struggled to his matchstick legs. "We carry our truncheons like flaming torches of justice. Bring light to the darkness of your savage streets," he croaked. "Follow that train!"

"What train?"

"The train with the Fumble Fortune, of course!"

Rump understood. "Are you saying it's been stolen? But that old man Urnip seemed such a nice old bloke."

"He won't get away from the flaming truncheons of Wildpool police. We always get our man. Inspector Beadle expects every man to do his duty!"

Driver Rump climbed back into his cab and pulled the wild-eyed, white-whiskered Constable Liddle after him.

The picture in the *Wildpool Bugle* newspaper showed the problem . . .

though you have already worked it out. The coal train was facing the wrong way. . .

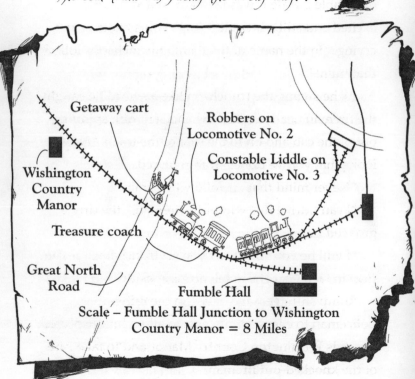

Getaway cart

Robbers on
Locomotive No. 2

Constable Liddle on
Locomotive No. 3

Wishington
Country
Manor

Treasure coach

Great North
Road

Fumble Hall

Scale – Fumble Hall Junction to Wishington
Country Manor = 8 Miles

"I'll have to run backwards," Driver Rump explained. "And we have a heavy load of coal trucks

to push ahead of us."

That's when a very unfortunate accident happened. There is not a lot of room on the footplate of a locomotive, and with Rump and his fireman and Constable Liddle it was pretty crowded. Liddle, excited and still a little dazed, drew his truncheon crying, "In the name of the flaming truncheons follow that train!"

As he swung the truncheon like a sword he caught the fireman neatly on the jaw and sent him spinning out of the cab and on to the side of the track. "Now look what you've done!" Rump roared.

"Never mind that . . . follow that train!"

"I can't drive this without a fireman," the driver groaned.

"I will be your fireman . . . your truncheons-of-fire-man in fact! Can you smell burning cloth?"

Rump shrugged and called to the railway policeman to change the points to allow him to reverse towards Wishington Country Manor and to take care of the knocked-out fireman.

By the time he was ready to leave he found Liddle shovelling coal into the firebox. "No, no, no!" he

cried. "We have enough steam already . . . you're damping down the fire." Sure enough the chimney of Locomotive No. 3 was pouring out sooty and sparking black smoke.

Rump waved to the guard at the far end of his train to release the brake and they began to roll down the hill. The weight of the coal trucks dragged them along but the choked engine was running out of steam. It was s-l-o-w.

Of course we know that the robbers were heading to a dead-end. No matter how long it took, Liddle and Rump would catch up to Locomotive No. 2 in the end.

Smiff and Samuel Dreep shivered as they sat at the crossing and waited. The sun was setting behind clouds as grey as slate. And the faces of the Crime Academy crew were grey too. The train was ten minutes late. They wore caps pulled down and scarves covered the bottom halves of their faces. It wasn't just the cold that made them wrap up their faces.

A man sat on a wooden stool by the side of the track and grinned the grin of a simpleton. He wasn't a simpleton – he was a trains-potter, but sometimes it's hard to tell them apart. "Afternoon," he said with a simpleton smile. "Are you trains-potting?"

"Er . . . yes," Smiff said.

"Always happy to meet another trains-potter. My name is Tarquin."

"Pleased to meet you, Tarquin," Smiff mumbled.

"Of course you don't usually see trains on this line," Tarquin the potter explained. "But there's a secret train due any time. I'm the only one that knows about it . . . well. Me and the Wildpool East Train Society . . . we call ourselves WETS."

"Good name," Smiff muttered into the scarf.

"Of course I had to take an afternoon off work to see this great occasion . . . the first train to run to Wishington Country Manor. I will report back to the WETS."

"Report what?" Dreep asked as he huddled inside his long coat.

"Report the number of the locomotive. Since Locomotive No. 1 exploded there are just Locomotive No. 2 and Locomotive No. 3 left. My guess is it will be Locomotive No. 2 or Locomotive No. 3. What do you reckon?"

"I reckon," Smiff said carefully, "that if that train don't get here soon I'm going to have to kill you before you bore me to death."

"Ha! Ha!" the simpleton . . . sorry, trains-potter . . . laughed. "Just as well I can see it coming then! Showing a clean, light grey smoke . . . sign of a good fireman that."

"Twelve minutes late," Dreep said. "I hope there haven't been problems."

Smiff and Dreep jumped quickly to the road, their freezing feet forgotten, and watched as the smoke trail turned into a locomotive and then they could see the treasure coach glowing yellow in the dying light of the day.

The track ran downhill to the spot where the Crime Academy cart waited at the crossing. Turnip had no brakes so the train was running too quickly and dashed past the waiting robbers.

Old Turnip threw the locomotive into reverse. The whole train clanked and shuddered and complained but it rolled back towards Dreep and Smiff. Still it was another four minutes wasted. They were sixteen minutes behind the planned time.

154

Dreep and Turnip tugged at the door to the treasure coach as Smiff backed the horse towards the line.

"Locomotive No. 2!" the trains-potter cried. "Wonderful! I have it in my book. The other WETS will be so-o jealous."

Each treasure chest was heavy but between them – the teacher, the highwayman and the pupils were able to load them both on to the cart.

"Now that is interesting . . . exciting even," Tarquin cried.

"What? We're not doing anything wrong. It's a delivery to a farm," Dreep said as he sweated over a chest full of gold.

"No, no, no!" the simpleton smiled. "I mean it is exciting to see *two* locomotives on the line at the same time."

"What are you on about?" Smiff grunted.

The trains-potter pointed with his pencil. "There's another locomotive heading this way. Thick, black smoke . . . poor firebox work is that. It'll be slow and it'll probably start fires by the side of the track! Careless. I wonder what number this one is?"

Smiff was sweating and nervous. "I don't suppose

155

it could be Locomotive No. 1, could it?"

"I doubt it . . . unless it's a ghost train."

"Then it's bleeding Locomotive No. 3 then, isn't it?" Smiff exploded.

"I think you may be right," the simpleton said . . . simply.

"The *real* question is . . . what's it bleeding doing here?" Smiff cried as the second chest of gold was lowered on to the cart and Rick Turnip began to cover both the chests with hay.

"No. The real question is, will it be able to stop in time before it hits this train. I mean, the driver has a guard's van and a row of coal trucks blocking his view. The coal trucks are heavy and the brake on the guard's van won't be strong enough to stop it in time . . . he's running backwards."

"So he throws it into forwards," Rick Turnip said. His eyes were fixed on the coal train that was just half a mile away now.

"Ah! No!" the trains-potter said, wagging his pencil. "That smoking fire won't be heating the boiler . . . there won't be enough steam to send the train forward. No. It looks like a disaster to me. Half a mile at thirty miles per hour – Ooooh! They'll smash into your train in two minutes. Anyone standing here will be killed on the spot! They won't know what hit them. Unless it's me, of course, I would know what hit me because I have been watching. But any passing stranger will be wiped out with flying wood, shredded by shards of metal or sizzled with streams of steam. . ."

But Samuel Dreep had stopped listening. "Climb aboard the cart, Mr Turnip!" he called and reached down a hand to help the old man aboard.

"Nancy!" Smitt called. "Hurry!"

"No, you get away," the brave girl cried. "Your cart is heavy. They can stop, jump off and walk after you. They'll soon catch you. They need to keep following the train."

"The trains-potter says it'll smash into you in two minutes!" Dreep moaned.

"A minute and a half now!" the young man said cheerfully.

"Not if I set away now!" Nancy cried. She threw the regulator to the right the way she'd seen Rick Turnip do and the train wheels skidded and screeched

on the iron rails. At last they found some grip and Locomotive No. 2 lurched forward.

"One minute," the trains-potter cried.

Smiff jumped off the cart and grabbed the horse's head-collar and led it down the road back to Wildpool. "Come on, you nag! You'll be dog-food . . . steam-cooked dog-food at that. . . Come on!"

The horse plodded slowly. Then Nancy yanked the rope that blew the whistle and the blast startled the horse into a fast trot. As it jogged past Smiff, Dreep reached down and pulled him on to the front seat of the cart. In moments they were safely clear and heading home down the darkening road.

Dreep looked back, horrified as he saw the coal train rumbling down towards the treasure train just as the trains-potter had said it would.

Nancy heaved at the regulator but the whistle blast had cost her a lot of steam.

On the coal train the clumsy coal clutter in the firebox began to burn through and make some steam again. Driver Rump threw the engine into forward.

"Thirty seconds!" the trains-potter clapped. "I can draw an on-the-spot picture for the WETS weekly magazine. I'll be famous! An eye witness!" He turned to a clean page on his number-collecting book and waited. "Twenty seconds," he gasped. He started drawing.

Nancy shovelled coal into the firebox of No. 2 and it began to pull away up the four-mile climb towards Wishington Country Manor.

"Ten seconds!"

The coal train slowed. Its wheels were whirring like an express train and the guard was heaving on the brake lever as if his life depended on it.

Maybe that's because his life did depend on it! The guard's van would be the first to smash into the treasure coach and the guard would be crushed like a spider under a steam hammer, a moth under a mallet or a butterfly under a bum.

Slithering on the evening-damp of the rails the coal wagons rocked, they slowed, they skidded by the trains-potter. "One second and. . ." And Locomotive No. 2 picked up just enough speed to pull away with its empty treasure coach.

The coal wagons crept past the man with the notebook. "We're looking for the Fumble Fortune!" Constable Liddle cried.

"They went that way!" the trains-potter shouted, pointing after Nancy's train.

"Didn't they unload the treasure here?" Rump asked. "We saw the train stop."

"No. They just dropped off farm supplies."

"Then the Fumble Fortune must still be on that train. They can't escape. Follow them!" Liddle said.

Rump shrugged. He signed for the guard to release the brake then used his precious steam to push his load up the hill, westwards towards Wishington Country Manor.

Nancy was half a mile ahead. She could jump off the train at the end of the line and be lost in the darkness of the park around the Country Manor before Constable Liddle arrived. He would need a truncheon of fire to search and he didn't really have one.

So Nancy should have been safe.

She *should* have been safe.

But. . .

160

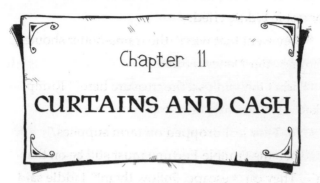

Chapter 11
CURTAINS AND CASH

4:00 p.m. Monday 27th February 1837

Nancy made a wonderful fireman.

She loved coal. She understood coal. She knew how it burned and could turn the rooms of Mayor Twistle's home toasty in minutes.

She could keep the water in Locomotive No. 2 bubbling as fast or as slow as Rick Turnip wanted.

But you know all that.

So why was Nancy heading for disaster when she was such a wonderful fireman?

I will tell you. Nancy was a fireman. She was not an engine driver.

She had watched the old highwayman pushing
the levers and changing the speed. But she had never
done it herself . . . until now.

And now she had no one to help. No one to tell
her what the levers and handles did, no one to tell her
what the dials and pointers meant.

And it was dark. She could only guess how far she
was from the buffers at the end of the line. The line
that led into the park of Wishington Country Manor.

Nancy let the fire go down and peered ahead. A
half-moon glinted on the tracks but that didn't help
much. She shut off the regulator and let the engine
coast along. But it was running light with only a
tender and an empty treasure coach to drag it back.

She saw the creamy stone building of Wishington
Country Manor looming ahead. Servants had already
lit candles in some of the rooms as they waited for
Lord Fumble to arrive.

The end of the line must be very near, she knew,
but the engine wasn't slowing enough. She needed to
throw the wheels into reverse but she wasn't sure how.

She looked over the side of the cab but couldn't
see the ground or the speed. If she jumped she could

break a leg and be caught.

"Oh, dear," she sighed. She hauled the rope and the screaming whistle let out the last of the steam from the boiler.

It also frightened seven badgers, thirty-nine crows, sixteen rabbits and six hundred and thirty-two worms half to death. It woke seventeen hedgehogs from hibernation and made Lord Fumble's cook drop a plate of pies on the kitchen floor. Let this be a lesson to you. Don't go whistling in the dark, no matter what they say.

The train slowed and she could tell from the creaky clanks it was safe to jump. She stood on the edge of the footplate. She peered down at the ground. She bent her knees, ready to jump.

And that was when Locomotive No. 2 hit the buffers.

Instead of being thrown off the cab Nancy was thrown forward. Her forehead smashed into the regulator lever.

It had been dark in the park but it was darker in Nancy's cracked skull.

*

The boiler of Locomotive No. 2 split but there was so little steam it didn't explode.

The treasure coach jumped off the track, twisted and rolled on its side, jamming the door shut.

Locomotive No. 3 crept carefully along and stopped just before it reached the wreckage. If Nancy was a poor driver then Mr Rump wasn't.

The coal train stopped. Constable Liddle climbed down stiffly to the track and hobbled towards the wreck of Locomotive No. 2. Driver Rump pulled a lantern from the front of his locomotive and followed.

"We've got the treasure coach anyway," the guard said, standing beside the yellow, crumpled coach.

"No we haven't," Driver Rump said.

"Lord Fumble will want his treasure," Constable Liddle said tugging at the twisted door. "If it's not in here then where's it gone?"

"It was unloaded when the train stopped at the main road," Rump said.

"That man by the roadside with a pencil . . . he said they unloaded farm supplies," Liddle reminded him.

Rump shook his head. "That carriage wasn't *carrying* any farm supplies. We were so keen to catch

this train we forgot that. They unloaded the treasure and by now they'll be in Wildpool hiding it. Lord Fumble won't see his fortune again."

"He won't be pleased," Liddle groaned. "Never mind. The Wildpool police always get their man. Let's arrest the driver and at least Inspector Beadle will be pleased."

The men walked along the track to the hissing Locomotive No. 2 and shone the lantern into the cab. Nancy lay there lifeless. "Yes, we have the thief."

"No," Rump said. "That's the fireman. The driver was an old man called Urnip . . . he must have jumped off at the roadside."

"Ohhhh! I don't care!" Liddle moaned. "So long as Inspector Beadle and Lord Fumble have *someone* to send to Darlham Gaol they won't mind. Help me get the lad on to the coal train and we'll take him back to Wildpool Police Station."

And so it was curtains for Nancy.

Curtains drop across the stage at the end of a show. Curtains mean "the end". Which is strange, because in the Apollo Music Hall the curtains

would soon be opening. As Smiff's granny used to say, "As one curtain closes another one opens". You can see Smiff's granny was a wise lady.

10 a.m. Tuesday 28th February 1837

In Wildpool Police Station there was joy the next morning. Inspector Beadle looked at his two officers. Liddle in his shredded uniform stood proudly in front of the station cell, a bandage wrapped round his burned bottom. Larch, rounder and redder and tidier, stood . . . almost as proud.

"The Wildpool police always get their man," Inspector Beadle said. "Except, in this case, it's not a man . . . it's a girl! Seems this Nancy posed as a boy to get a job on the railway."

The three men looked through the bars. Nancy sat quietly on the hard bench that served as a bed. A bandage round her head slipped over one eye. She did her best to look stupid.

"We know you were working with the driver," Inspector Beadle said. "The other driver, Rump – the one that trained you – says your friend's name was Urnip. Is that correct?"

"I think so," Nancy said.

"So this is who we are looking for," Constable Larch said and unrolled a poster.

WANTED
DEAD OR ALIVE
(OR SOMETHING IN BETWEEN)

X URNIP – THE TRAIN ROBBER
WANTED FOR
ROBBING THE FUMBLE FORTUNE. THIS MAN IS A MASTER OF DISGUISE. HE MAY APPEAR AS A RAILWAY WORKER OR HE MAY NOT.

REWARD OF HALF A CROWN FOR HIS CAPTURE

"Is that picture a good likeness?" Beadle asked.

"I don't think so," Nancy lied. "I was just a trains-potter. Urnip asked me if I wanted to join him – learn to drive. Of course I said yes! But I always had the feeling the grey hair was a wig. I reckon he's about twenty years old."

Liddle and Larch groaned. "So we wouldn't spot him if we stood next to him in the tavern!" Larch sighed.

"Wouldn't spot who?" a quiet voice asked. The policemen swung round to see Lord Fumble standing in the doorway to the cells.

"This Urnip, my lord," Beadle said, showing the poster.

"Torture the prisoner. Get him to talk," the furious-faced Fumble spat.

"It's a girl, sir. She disguised herself as a boy to get a job on the footplate. She'd never met Urnip before."

"And you *believe* her, you idiot?" Lord Fumble sneered. "I knew I'd seen that face before when I saw her on the platform at Fumble Hall. I *said* I knew the face. Didn't I?"

"Yes, Lord Fumble," Nancy whispered.

"It is the face I sentenced to forty years in Darlham Gaol. It is a Turnip face." He jabbed a fat finger at the girl. "You are one of the Turnip family, aren't you?

Rick Turnip's granddaughter?"

"The granddaughter of his mother's brother," she said.

"And the driver?" Lord Fumble went on. "The real criminal mastermind behind this is your great-uncle, Rick Turnip. He was released from the gaol just a week ago and he's back to his old tricks. Isn't that true, you young villain?"

"No, Lord Fumble," Nancy said.

The lord shrugged his wide shoulders. "If we don't find the driver then you'll be the one to hang!"

Inspector Beadle was even larger than Lord Fumble and he rolled forward to block the lord's view of the cell. "Sorry, my lord, but the courts would never allow her to hang. They may transport her to Australia for seven years but no court would hang the child."

"The court *will* hang her if *I* am the judge," Fumble laughed. "And I am magistrate tomorrow. Have her brought before me." He swung round on the two constables. "And you two . . . go out and search every rat's nest between here and Darlham till you find Rick Turnip."

He stumped out of the police station and into his waiting carriage.

"You heard him," Inspector Beadle said to his constables and he turned and waddled down the stairs to his office.

Next door to the police station stood Master Crook's Crime Academy. The mood was of gloom . . . and rage.

Alice ripped the letter down from the noticeboard and waved it at Samuel Dreep, Smiff and Rick Turnip. "Have you seen this? Have you *seen* it?"

They nodded silently.

MASTER CROOK'S CRIME ACADEMY

To all students and staff.

As you know one of our new pupils, Nancy Turnip, has been arrested while taking part in the Great Train Robbery. This is very sad and a lesson to us all. Nancy was told to abandon the train after the Fumble Fortune had been unloaded at the Great North Road. Nancy chose to disobey. She carried on and was arrested. This puts the whole Academy in danger.

In future all plots made by Master Crook must be obeyed to the letter. There must be no attempt to rescue Nancy. Plans to give away the Fumble Fortune must go ahead.

M Crook

"What a RAT!" Alice screamed. "You don't just abandon your mates! I'm going to take this letter and stick it up Master Crook's crooked nose."

"If his nose is crooked you won't get the letter very far," Smiff said.

Alice glared at the boy. She blew down the message tube in the wall. "Are you there, Master *Rat*?" she shouted. There was no reply. She ran to the door that led to the cellar and clattered down, two steps at a time.

The heavy curtain hung there as lifeless as a hanged thief. She took a deep breath. She stepped forward. She pulled the curtain aside. There was a wide chair there. Behind the chair was a plain wooden door.

Alice tried the door handle. The door was locked. "Master Crook?" the girl shouted. "Are you there? Come on out. I want a word or two."

The only answer Alice got was silence.

6:00 p.m. Tuesday 28th February 1837

The poster outside the Apollo Music Hall was freshly pasted on and flapped in the chill evening wind . . .

APOLLO MUSIC HALL, WILDPOOL

SOLE LESSEE MR FARLAND

...Y PRESENTS

TONIGHT'S PERFORMANCE CANCELLED

PRIVATE EVENT FOR WILDPOOL AND HELTON RAILWAY COMPANY

SHAREHOLDERS ONLY

PRESENT YOUR SHARE CERTIFICATE TO GAIN ENTRY

Customers who bought tickets for

THE TERRIFIC TORINOS' TALKING TURKEY ACT

will have their money refunded. Apologies for this short notice

Live in conversation

No dogs, no drinking your own drink, no spitting and ladies are
not allowed to smoke
Food and drink are served at the intervals, before and after the show

The heavy velvet curtains swung open. The drama
began.

"Good evening, shareholders," Samuel Dreep cried

from the stage. He stood behind a table. On the table rested lists of names. Treasure chests stood on the platform beside him with bags of coins inside. "I am Andrew Brown of the Fumble Estates," Dreep lied. He wore a gingery wig and eyeglasses to change the way he looked. But nothing could disguise the fine, fluttering fingers of the Crime Academy teacher.

Smiling Smiff and sulking Alice stood beside him, ready to help.

Some of the audience gave a patter of applause. Dreep raised his tall hat, bowed a little and went on. "Lord Fumble sent me to thank you for the faith you have shown in the great railway plan. . ."

"We don't want thanks, we want some money!" a woman shouted.

"I know," Dreep nodded. "It will be three years before the main line reaches this far north."

"Three years!" a man roared. "We'll have starved and be in our graves before then!"

Dreep held up his hands for silence. "Lord Fumble knows this . . . and this is why he has decided to pay a *dividend* from the money the railway is making."

173

"But last month he said the railway wasn't making money!" the woman cried.

"The coal trade from Helton Colliery to Wildpool river drops has done well. Lord Fumble thinks it is only fair that you should have a share. . ."

"How much?" the man called.

Dreep took a deep breath . . . a Dreep breath. "A thousand pounds," he said.

There was a moment of stunned silence then a ragged cheer, cries of excitement. It took ten minutes to die down. "You get this cash now . . . *and* you keep your share certificates. When the railway starts to pay in three years', time you will, of course, get regular money from it. Now, if you would like to line up my assistants will make sure everyone with a share gets their cash!"

Excited and happy people joined the queue and carried away their cash. Mrs Mixly clung to her husband's arm as he proudly showed his certificate ... the last thing in their house. "It's roast beef and plum pudding for dinner tonight, my dears," she told the twins.

The last in line was a man with a scarf wrapped

around his face. "And last, but not least," Samuel Dreep smiled, "we have your share, Andrew Brown."

"Hush!" the estate manager hissed. "No one must know how I helped you. Lord Fumble mustn't know I told you about his plans to move the treasure."

"You're a good man, Andrew. No one *shall* know."

Brown grinned. "And Lord Fumble wants no one to know he had that million pounds while the shareholders starved. It would make him unpopular – no one would trust him ever again. He wants people to think it was just about ten pounds in the chests."

"So, let the world think that," Dreep nodded.

"There's still money in the chest," Smiff pointed out.

Dreep nodded. "That will meet the costs of Master Crook's Crime Academy," the teacher said.

"But it won't meet the cost of Nancy's life if she hangs tomorrow, will it?" Alice spat. "All the money in the world won't pay for that."

The girl pulled her shawl around her shoulders and stormed off into the Wildpool winds that failed to cool the burning bitterness growing in her heart.

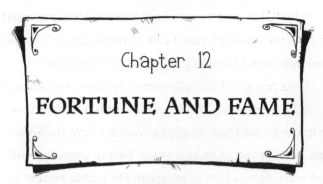

Chapter 12

FORTUNE AND FAME

Wildpool Court – Wednesday 1ˢᵗ March 1837

Nancy stood quietly in the court, chained to the "dock".

The court was full with reporters. The first great train robbery would be news around the world.

The clerk of the court was still the same fussy little man with spectacles and a bald head. But now he was eighty years old or more – ten years older than Lord Fumble. "Court will rise for the judge!"

Lord Fumble was dressed in the finest, scarlet judge's robes and a wig as wide as the doorway.

Did you know, these wide wigs are called "Full-bottomed" wigs? Fat Lord Fumble had a

full-bottomed wig and a full-bottomed bottom. A matching pair!

His face wore a vicious smirk. Someone was going to suffer.

"What are the charges?"

"Highway robbery, I suppose, your honour," the clerk said. "It's hard to say. No one has ever robbed a train before. I'm not sure if there is a law against it."

"There is now," Fumble snarled. He glared at Nancy. "Do you plead guilty?"

A man in a short white wig and black gown jumped to his feet. "My client wishes to plead not guilty, your honour."

Fumble turned his red face towards him. "And who are *you*? And how can a gutter-girl like *that* afford a lawyer to defend her?"

"My name is Dreep, your honour," Samuel Dreep said, bowing. "Friends of the accused have paid for her defence."

Fumble leaned forward and said quietly in a soft but rasping voice for Dreep's ears only, "It will do her no good. No one steals my money and gets away with it."

Dreep bowed and smiled. "May I call a witness?"

"Call as many as you like. You are wasting your time and mine."

"Call Constable Liddle of the Wildpool Police Force," Dreep said.

"Call Constable Liddle!" the little, bald clerk echoed.

Liddle stepped into the witness stand, took an oath and looked at the judge nervously.

You will be pleased to know Liddle was dressed in a new uniform and helmet. He had spent an hour shining his buttons.

"You are a hero of the Wildpool Police Force," the judge said. "Get someone sent to prison for this dreadful crime and there may be a medal in it for you!"

"Thank you, sir," Liddle said.

"Constable," Dreep cut in before the judge could offer to pay the man a hundred pounds to lie. "Did you see Nancy Turnip take any money?"

"No, sir, but I did see her mess about with the carriage coupling."

"Did you see her pass treasure chests to friends at the Great North Road?"

"No, sir, but. . ."

"The treasure was loaded on to a cart on the evening of the robbery," Dreep said.

"We did see a cart drive away before we reached the road. . ."

"But Nancy Turnip didn't go with it, did she?"

"No, sir, but. . ."

"Because Nancy Turnip is innocent. She was paid as a fireman on the locomotive. She did as she was told. The driver told her to stop, she stopped. The driver escaped and Nancy set off to finish the journey to Wishington Country Manor. She knew nothing about a robbery."

Constable Liddle shrugged his thin and rounded shoulders. "If you say so, sir."

Lord Fumble crashed a fist into the bench in front of him. "NOT if he *says* so!" he roared and his eyes were red with rage. "This girl is one of the evil Turnip family. The driver was her great-uncle – a man who has just been released after forty years in Darlham Gaol and who will go straight back there if I get my

hands on him. *Someone* has to be punished for this crime!" He placed a black cap carelessly on his head and began to read the death sentence. . . "The court orders you to be taken from here to the place from where you came."

"Sorry, my lord," the old clerk said quickly, "but you cannot hang a child for stealing ten pounds. . ."

"It wasn't ten pounds it was . . . it was. . . " Lord Fumble stopped himself. He watched as the reporters held their pencils in the air, ready to write down what he said. "It . . . it *was* . . . ten pounds," he growled. "But I can sentence the girl to be transported, can't I? Just for being one of the Turnip clan she deserves that! Pass me a charge sheet. . ."

"My lord!" Dreep cried.

"Silence in court or I'll have you packed off with the girl."

Dreep sat and buried his head in his hands, helpless.

In the gallery a girl struggled to rise to her feet and scream, "It's not fair," but a boy with shaggy black hair held her down. "Not now, Alice . . . you'll get us all arrested."

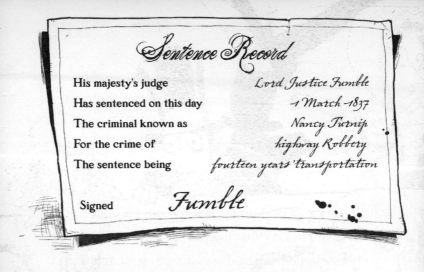

"Take her down," the judge ordered.

"The court will rise!" the bald clerk cried.

A figure dressed as an old woman in a shawl rose to its feet and threw back the shawl. "Wait!" the figure cried.

Lord Fumble peered at the figure and a slow smile spread across his fat lips. "Ahhh! My old friend Rick Turnip." The judge turned to Constable Liddle. "Arrest that man."

"Sorry, my worship, but me handcuffs are on the girl," Liddle said.

"Well . . . well . . . take them *off* the girl and get them on that thug!"

Liddle unlocked the handcuffs and moved towards Rick Turnip.

"Take one step and the girl gets it!" the highwayman cried. Under the shawl he pointed a finger at Alice White who was sitting next to him. "This pistol is loaded and I'm not afraid to use it," the old man said.

Alice had a brain as sharp as any needle. "Help! Oh, help! Don't let him shoot me, sir! I is as innocent as the day is short. I ain't done nothing to deserve to die young. I beg you, do as he says!"

"Wait!" Lord Fumble ordered Constable Liddle. He turned towards his old enemy Turnip. "If you shoot the girl you *will* hang this time. Put the gun down."

"Not till you set Nancy free."

Fumble raised his massive shoulders. "I will set Nancy free when I get the person that took the Fumble Fortune."

Rick Turnip lowered his finger. He took a deep breath. "That was me, your honour. I planned it all and I did the robbery. The girl trusted me because I am her great-uncle. But she knew nothing about it. Let her go. Take me instead."

Lord Fumble slowly raised the Sentence Record, crumpled it into a ball and threw it on the floor. He smiled at the newspaper reporters. "This is a great day

for justice in this land! Lord Fumble has arrested one of the most famous highwaymen ever to plague our roads."

"Oh, thanks, your honour!" Rick Turnip blushed as Liddle snapped the handcuffs on the thin old wrists.

"This man is so cunning he even invented a new crime – a crime so new there is no punishment for it!" Lord Fumble roared on as a dozen pencils scratched away at a dozen notepads. "Where is my fortune? The Fumble Fortune?" he asked.

"The wheel fell off the getaway cart, my lord," Turnip sighed. "It rolled off Wildpool Bridge and sank to the bottom of the river. All ten pounds of it."

Lord Fumble gave his old enemy a look of pure poison. "So, Rick Turnip, terror of the trains, I hereby sentence you to. . ."

A hush fell over the court. A dozen pencils hung in the air over a dozen waiting sheets of paper.

"I sentence you to forty years in Darlham Gaol!"

A gasp ran around the court. Samuel Dreep jumped to his feet. "I object to the harshness. . ."

"It's all right," Rick Turnip said cheerfully. "*I* don't object. Take me away, Constable! I'm going home."

AFTERWORD

The rap on the Mixly door was heavy as an axe. Mrs Mixly skipped down the hall and threw open the door. "Mr Candy! Mr Knuckle! How nice to see you!" she cried. "Come in out of the cold and warm yourself by the fire," she said and led the way into the living room. A warm fire of coal and logs crackled in the grate. A fine stew full of best beef stood on the new table and two cheerful children were helping themselves.

Even the light was warm and butter-yellow from a crowd of candles.

Candy looked unsure. "We've come for the hundred pounds."

"We've spent a hundred on the new furniture to replace the old stuff you took away," Mrs Mixly said and fluttered her eyes prettily at Knuckle. "But this new stuff is so much nicer, don't you think?"

"If you've spent the money then we'll have to take

something else. I did say we'd take the children and sell them to a chimney sweep," Knuckle said with a cruel smile. He grabbed Martin in one huge hand and Millie with the other.

"Wait," Mrs Mixly cried and she moved towards the kitchen door. She opened it carefully and stood there. "Are you saying that if I don't pay you one hundred pounds you will take my children away?"

"Exactly," Knuckle chuckled.

"Couldn't put it better myself," Candy agreed.

"I think that is called 'demanding money with menaces' and I think it is against the law, you naughty boys," Mrs Mixly said.

"Hah!" Candy sneered. "Like we care, eh, Knuckle?"

"Like we care," his partner agreed.

"But Inspector Beadle cares, don't you?" Mrs Mixly's voice trilled. "Don't you?"

The light from the kitchen was blocked by a shadow as the huge form of Beadle loomed into view. "I care," Beadle said. "And I am arresting you. There'll be no more bringing misery to the poor."

Knuckle and Candy cringed like cowardly cats faced by bulldog Beadle.

"Oh, sir! We was only doing our job!" Candy cried.

"You didn't have to enjoy it so much," Beadle said. "Liddle? Larch!" The two constables appeared. "Take them away."

Rick Turnip's faded eyes glowed like jewels. He unwrapped the latest parcel from the Darlham book shop. The magazine was crinkly fresh and the old man stroked it with love. "What have you got there, my old friend?" the governor of Darlham Gaol asked.

"A new story by that young writer, Charles Dickens. His *Pickwick Papers* was wonderful, but this looks even better! *The Adventures of Oliver Twist – Or the Parish Boy's Progress. Part 1.* I think this young Dickens can become a great writer."

The governor chuckled. "You should know. I've never known anyone read as much as you, Rick!"

"Yes," the old man nodded looking at the sketches. "It was quite nice in the outside world. . . I have a wonderful niece called Nancy . . . a brave girl. She's promised to visit as often as she can. And the young people at the Crime Academy were great. But I missed my library."

The governor nodded. "And we've missed you. Now, I'm sorry to spoil your *Oliver Twist* treat but we've a couple of young men just arrived. They are really upset – sentenced to two years in here. They look pretty terrified, to be honest."

Turnip the Highwayman rose to his feet. "Leave them to me. We'll soon have them so busy they'll forget their misery. What are they called?"

"Candy and Knuckle," the governor said.

"I'll have them right as rain in no time," the old man promised.

They walked down the cold corridors together. "It's good to have you back, Rick."

"It's good to be home, governor."

In the gloom of the room below the Crime Academy, Alice sat and faced the curtain. It moved as the door opened behind and the wide chair creaked as Master Crook sat in it.

"I'm not saying sorry," Alice said.

The sigh from behind the curtain was enough to make the walls tremble. "But *I am* saying sorry, Alice."

"What?"

"I was wrong. You were right. There is a copy of the Crime Academy school rules on the noticeboard upstairs. . ."

"I seen it."

"Add a new one to the bottom, Alice."

And that's what she did . . .

MASTER CROOK'S CRIME ACADEMY
SCHOOL RULES

Pupils must ...

1 Run in ye corridors at all times
2 Be late for ye lessons
3 Disobey ye teachers
4 Write on ye school walls
5 Shout ye out aloud
6 Cheat in ye tests
7 Eat in ye class
8 Pick ye nose and eat ye it
9 Damage ye books or carve ye names on ye desk

BUT:

10 Pupils must **NOT** pick on other pupils. No matter how weedy and worthless a classmate looks they all have a place at Master Crook's. Be warned. Bully not or ye shall be bullied.

11 PUPILS OF MASTER CROOK'S CRIME ACADEMY LOOK OUT FOR ONE ANOTHER.

Lord Fumble sat in Wishington Country Manor. The room was decorated in hand-painted wallpaper with birds and trees, the curtains were rich velvet and the windows wide and bright. The ceilings were cream plaster, moulded to look like grapes, and the furniture was the richest in the land. It was like a fairy-tale palace of your dreams. But the old man was miserable. He didn't see the beauty. He only saw his empty treasure chest.

Driver Rump stood in front of his lordship and showed him a map. "There you are, my lord. The main line will be passing to the west of Wildpool in no time at all. We need to link up to it."

"I can't afford to build any more railway," the fat lord snarled.

"If you sell me the company then I will find people to put in the money . . . but I won't cheat them the way you did," Rump said.

"I'll sell it for million pounds," Lord Fumble said.

Driver Rump turned to the young man by his side. "Well, Tarquin, what do you think?"

"I think he owes a million to the men who built the tracks and the stations – the people who made the

three locomotives, Dad. And there's only one of them still running. The person who buys the railway will start out a million ponds in debt."

Rump shrugged. "See, your lordship? You owe a million pounds. The collectors will be knocking on your door and taking away your furniture soon. They may even have you locked in Darlham Gaol for debt."

"Not that!" his lordship groaned. "I'll sell! Pay me half a million."

Tarquin stepped forward and looked at the notepad in his hand. It was the notepad he used to collect locomotive numbers. "I've worked it out," he said. "The Wildpool and Helton Railway is worth . . . one pound. Sell it to us for one pound, Lord Fumble, or go to Darlham Gaol."

Lord Fumble looked in his empty treasure chest. Finally he spat, "Agreed."

Driver Rump turned to his son. "There you are, lad! You own the biggest train set in the world!"

"A trains-potter's dream," Tarquin the trains-potter smiled.

Samuel Dreep answered the door. Mrs Mixly stood there with a twin in either hand.

"Master Crook?"

The young teacher spread his hands wide. "No. I am not Master Crook, but maybe I can help you?"

"The other day a girl from here was amazingly kind to us."

"That would be Alice," Dreep nodded.

"I would like my Millie and Martin to grow up like that. I wonder if I can enrol them in the Crime Academy?" the woman asked.

"It would be a pleasure. All they have to do is

fail a simple test."

"Fail? Most schools want you to pass."

"But this is not like most schools," Dreep said.

And that was the truth.

28 February 1901

*Outside my window the children are skipping.
I don't suppose they know what the song is
really about. But I do. And you do.*

Ricky Turnip robbed the train
Highway robber, mighty brain
Ricky Turnip, poor and humble
Stole the fortune from Lord Fumble

Ricky Turnip is no good
Chop him up for fire wood
If the fire won't burn his head
Use his wooden arm instead.

Yes, yes, I know . . . the last bit confuses Rick with the famous Tom Turnip. But Rick Turnip wouldn't mind that.

In fact, he'd quite like it don't you think?

LOOK OUT FOR MORE

MASTER CROOK'S
CRIME ACADEMY

ESCAPADES COMING SOON!

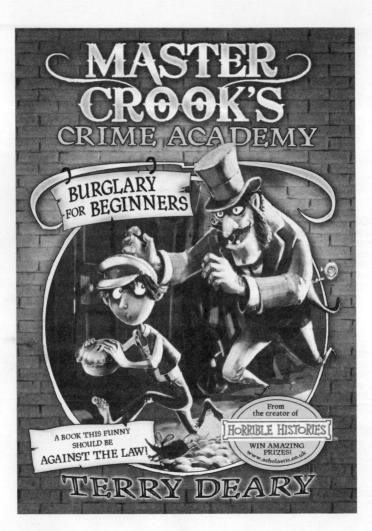

MASTER CROOK'S CRIME ACADEMY

WHERE SCOUNDRELS SAVE THE DAY. . .

Mayor Twistle is one of the richest men in Wildpool. But when it comes to helping the poor, his hands are kept firmly in his pockets. It's about time the tables were turned!

On the other side of town, Smiff Smith is enrolling at the world's first Crime Academy. He knows his life will never be the same again, but he has no idea the adventures that lie in store — or the danger he's about to face!

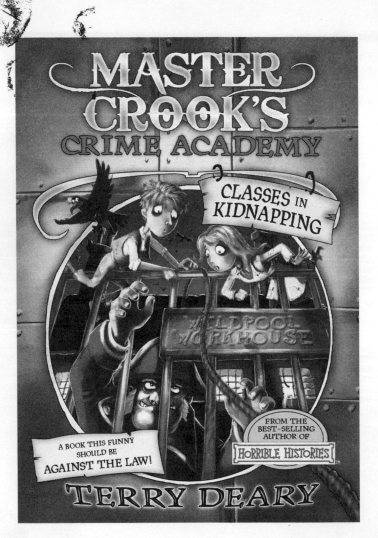

MASTER CROOK'S
CRIME ACADEMY

WHERE SCOUNDRELS SAVE THE DAY. . .

The doors to Wildpool's first workhouse are now open and Mr and Mrs Humble run it with iron fists. So much so that the poor would rather be back on the streets!

With the help of a few disguises, a lesson in ransom notes and most importantly . . . a hostage – the academy's students are ready for another adventure!